Moving Day

Moving Day

Euthena M. Newman

Library of Congress Control Number: 2020919255
ISBN: Hardcover   978-1-6641-3488-1
               Softcover   978-1-6641-3487-4
               eBook   978-1-6641-3486-7

Print information available on the last page.

Rev. date: 11/04/2020

To order additional copies of this book, contact:
Xlibris
844-714-8691
www.Xlibris.com
Orders@Xlibris.com
819714

CONTENTS

ACKNOWLEDGMENTS

WRITING MY FIRST novel has been challenging as well as rewarding. First of all, I want to thank God for giving me the desire, the inspiration, and the skill necessary to undertake such a task. Through the course of writing this book, I encountered many persons who knowingly and unknowingly inspired me to bring this book to completion. And to a few of them, I offer words of thanks.

To my son, Damon Newman, Sr. — I continue to be amazed at your clarity of understanding during our passionate conversations. You never doubted.

To my grandchildren, Damon Jr, Amani, Khania, Jada — You are my inspiration for all that I do. I know that you will do greater things because of the light of your life.

To my siblings, Buddy, Blanche, Justine, Beverly, LaVerne — I could not have asked for a greater family. You five have always been my anchor and my greatest cheerleaders.

I am grateful to my pastor, Dr. Kevin A. Williams, who supplied the extra push I needed to stay the course when he issued a time sensitive challenge to stop procrastinating and complete those unfinished projects.

A special thanks is reserved for Ms. Polly Sowell, my twelfth-grade English teacher, who taught me how to write with power and conviction and would not accept anything less.

And to my many friends — You helped shape my ideas and were my constant companions every step of the way.

To everyone I may have forgotten who directly or indirectly moved with me along this journey, I am eternally indebted.

To my sweet mother, Rosie Miller Newman, whose words of wisdom are the threads that continue to repair the tapestry of my life. Love has no boundaries.

PROLOGUE

EVERYTHING IN THE universe moves. The earth moves around the sun, the moon revolves around the earth, and water flows over and under the earth. Life itself is a continuous series of movements.

We move from the womb to the world and from childhood to adulthood and on through middle age and finally to old age. When we stop moving, we die. The time we move, the way we move, where we move, and who and what we encounter as we move dictate our life narratives.

This is the story of four women and their movements through life. Although their family trajectories were different, they found each other at the time when they were transitioning from adolescence to adulthood. The friendship that was forged became eternal because, from the beginning, they were intentional in sharing all their joys and sorrows. They never let one of their group move alone.

CHAPTER 1

A Pleasant Recollection
of Past Events

CHARLOTTE TIMMONS WRIGHT was gently awoken by the sweet melody offered by a family of songbirds that had taken up residence in the old oak tree that stood just outside her bedroom window. For a split second, she wanted to stay in bed and spend eternity beneath her warm covers, but she quickly remembered how grateful she was just to be able to move at her age. Once fully conscious, she sat up in bed and whispered her usual prayer.

"Thank you, God, for letting me rise this morning, and I hope to be able to rise tomorrow morning." She knew it was a repetitious prayer, but it was one that came directly from her heart each time.

Charlotte sat immobile a few moments longer until her mind convinced her body it was time to move. Once out of bed, she rushed, as much as she could, across the room to close the window and reached for her robe; she then wrapped it around her body a little tighter than usual. Although it was the middle of June, the crisp morning air that came through the open window seemed to go right to her bones. But what else do you expect from a seventy-eight-year-old woman on blood thinners?

"If you think seventy-eight is bad, wait till you turn eighty. You pray to get old, but you never think you'll get broke down." Charlotte imagined hearing her mother's sweet voice admonishing her from the other side.

Well, Charlotte felt a little "broke down" herself this morning as she stretched her fingers and rubbed her knees to get the juices flowing.

"And good morning to you, Arthur" was the greeting Charlotte gave to her invisible but always unwelcome visitor as she rubbed her knees and shoulders on her way to the bathroom.

She seemed to be moving slower and slower these days.

Standing in front of the bathroom mirror, she took a good look at herself. Then she smiled.

"Mama, I thought you left me years ago, but I can still see you looking back at me in this mirror."

After a brief pause, Charlotte exclaimed, "Mama, I really *have* turned into you! I even have your eyes and neck!"

As Charlotte tried to smooth out the wrinkled skin under her chin, she noted her ever thinning gray hair and the deep lines in her face that were made by keeping secrets shared only with good friends.

Charlotte completed her morning routine. She washed her face, brushed her teeth, combed her hair, and recorded her weight, blood pressure, and glucose level before counting out her daily pills—all eight of them.

Even so, she had to admit that life was good.

After a nice warm bath with lavender oil, she moisturized her skin with the shea butter that her daughter had shipped to her straight from Accra, Ghana. Charlotte prepared her breakfast: a tall glass of tempered spring water, a spinach and mushroom omelet, a cup of lemon and herb tea, and a bowl of steel-cut oatmeal with bananas, walnuts, and a dash of cinnamon. Although a loss of appetite is a natural part of aging, Charlotte's was still as robust as ever.

Her breakfast table was always set with her best Lenox china, Waterford crystal, and the antique silver flatware that was her mother's pride. Only 100 percent linen napkins ever graced her table, along with fresh flowers from her garden that she arranged in the tiny vase made by Isabella's little hands many years ago.

"If you don't treat yourself well, nobody else will" was her mother's motto.

Charlotte never rushed her breakfast. It was her favorite meal of the day. She always ended with a good cup of her special coffee, which was usually laced with a little heavy crème, a sprinkling of cinnamon, and a dash of Frangelico hazelnut liqueur.

As Charlotte stood in front of her kitchen window at the break of dawn, sipping on the last of her morning coffee, she remembered with a smile the words her great grandson would say when he wanted to get out of bed early on those Saturdays she wanted to sleep in, *"the sun is awake"*. The sun was indeed awake and it was the perfect time of day when Charlotte's thoughts were clearer and not shadowed by the cares of life. Just then she noticed the deafening quiet that seemed to blanket the entire house and Charlotte sighed, *this old house is just too big and too quiet. It is time to move.*

Bella and DJ, as she affectionately called her children, had paid little attention to their mother when she mentioned months ago the idea that she was considering "giving up housekeeping." The two of them were married with families of their own, and Dawson Sr., the one love of her life, was dead. The upkeep of the house had become unmanageable—even with a housekeeper and a gardener. She did not have the motivation or the energy to keep such a large house alive. It was aging faster than she was. Botox, she learned, cannot turn back the hands of time, and neither can a fresh coat of paint make an old house new. The house had become a cross. And Grandma Beulah always said, "If anything becomes a cross, get rid of it."

So six months ago, Charlotte resolved to get rid of her cross.

She decided to downsize but definitely not downgrade. Charlotte no longer needed the 3,500-square-foot, five-bedroom, house with a wraparound porch, but she did not want to give up all her amenities, such as her gourmet kitchen with warming drawers, her walk-in spa tub, and her heated bathroom floors. And there was her wonderful garden. When Dr. Dawson Wright first bought the house and carried his bride over the threshold, the lawn and surrounding grounds were lush and green and neatly trimmed and landscaped but void of color. Over the last forty years, Charlotte had practically dug up all the grass herself and transformed the nondescript grounds into an English-cottage garden, complete with waterfalls, sculptures, and a variety of fragrant flowers.

There were even some fruit trees. Spectacular and fragrant red roses partnered with lavender dianthus surrounded an oversize water fountain anchored in a reflecting pool. Charlotte intentionally selected plants that served as oases for pollinators because her mother loved butterflies. Symmetrical paved walkways ran throughout the grounds, providing a simple path toward the many flower beds, the small vegetable garden, and the wood-burning firepit that Dawson and DJ built together. The garden itself was bordered on all sides by tall flowering hedges that were perfectly manicured and enhanced the grounds' natural appeal. Charlotte often retired to the garden with a book and a cup of tea, and whenever a butterfly came near, she could almost feel her mother's presence.

Locating a suitable dwelling for downsizing but not downgrading had proven to be quite a challenge. Charlotte visited several properties with names such as retirement village, senior living, independent living, and the dreaded continuing care retirement community. They all meant, according to her friend Florence, that you were being "put out to pasture."

Then three weeks ago, while waiting in her podiatrist's office, Charlotte saw a colorful brochure that announced a new senior community—*The Gardens at the Manor. Nice name,* she thought. There were no pictures of depressing or decrepit-looking old people on the cover. Charlotte discretely put the brochure in her bag to view later. Summer was approaching, and she wanted her toes to be "sandals-ready," as her granddaughter Railynn often cautioned. She had a standing appointment at the local nail shop for a manicure but no pedicure. Since becoming diabetic, she only allowed a trained medical professional to come near her feet with a cutting instrument. After the podiatrist cut and filed her toenails, she still wanted someone else to make them look pretty. Her friend Vivian had recommended a wonderful nail technician named Courtney who made house calls and whose foot messages had become legendary. Charlotte had a standing appointment with her.

After Courtney left that evening, Charlotte remembered the brochure she put in her purse, retrieved it, and went online to investigate *The Gardens at the Manor.* She found the homeowner-reviews section, and suspiciously, each one was extremely positive. Charlotte called the contact number on the back of the brochure and made an appointment to check it out for herself.

The next day, after her morning health-care ritual and a hearty breakfast, Charlotte headed out for *The Gardens at the Manor*. With a copy of the directions printed from her computer on the passenger seat, she put the destination in her car's GPS. Bella never understood why her mother needed to print driving directions when she had a state-of-the-art GPS in her car. But Charlotte believed in having a backup.

"Never put all your eggs in one basket," she would remind Bella.

Charlotte would always arrive at any destination with at least twenty minutes to spare. Bella also thought this practice was antiquated. Charlotte explained that she always built in a safety net of at least twenty minutes in case she forgot to take a pot off the stove and had to turn around or if traffic was unusually heavy or for some other unforeseen occurrence. She never wanted to be late and thought it inconsiderate to have anyone waiting for her.

Charlotte arrived at her destination with time to spare. A security guard greeted her at the gate, verified her appointment, checked her identification, and invited her in. Charlotte proceeded along a brick driveway lined with white gardenias that were nestled among the most prolific and sweetest-smelling Carolina jessamine vines she had ever seen. The resident manager, a young lady who appeared to be around twenty-five years of age, greeted her with the warmest of smiles, reminiscent of a time when respect was a natural expectation, and proceeded to give her a most pleasant guided tour of the residence.

Charlotte instantly fell in love with the place. *The Manor*, as it was commonly called, had a day spa, a beauty shop, and a library (yes, with hardbound books as well as audio and digital copies) and a heated pool—all the amenities a woman of her age had come to appreciate. Each unit had a sunroom that allowed in just the right amount of light to nourish her precious seventy-five-year-old *Sansevieria trifasciata*, which had been her Grandma Beulah's. There was even a little garden plot at the back for those with green thumbs. In addition to the twenty-four-hour guard, cameras were strategically located on virtually every tree and light post throughout the grounds. *The Manor* was as secure as any property could be in these turbulent times. All that was left for Charlotte and the resident manager to discuss was cost.

When she got home, Charlotte reviewed her financial portfolio. She calculated that she could afford to stay at the *Manor* for at least twenty years, if her health permitted. By then, she would be in her late nineties and if she lived longer than that, then it would be Bella and DJ's call.

She could not wait to tell Stella, Florence, and Vivian about her visit and let them know she found the perfect place to downsize—and no, Vivian, she would not have to downgrade.

That was six months ago, and this morning, everything was boxed and ready for the movers except for those things too precious to trust with the hands of strangers. She would be transporting them personally in her black Mercedes-Benz E500 with cranberry-red interior, a birthday present from Dawson that she drove now only occasionally. Charlotte poured herself a fresh cup of her "special coffee" and began carefully packing the last of her mementos. When she opened a particularly unique envelope, an old faded picture of four happy-looking young girls greeted her. As she focused her eyes on the picture, she smiled as she recognized the familiar scene. She took a long, intense look at the faded photograph and remembered it was taken on the evening before their college graduation. Memories of that night rushed by so fast and clear that she could almost smell the Jean Nate perfume she was wearing and hear the Commodores' "Brick House" playing in the background. She could see Stella "taking the floor," her fluid, rhythmic dancing causing others to stop, step back, and watch. No one could do the Bump like Stella and Ray.

Charlotte carefully leaned back in her recliner, smiled, took a long and deep sip from her cup, and with closed eyes, was transported back to the day of their college graduation.

CHAPTER 2

On the Precipice of Adulthood

FOUR LONG YEARS seemed to have rushed by, and graduation day had finally arrived. Vivian shouted above the music coming from the radio as she picked up wet towels off the bathroom floor, "I hope this is the last time I have to share a bathroom with you women. Does anyone ever pick up after themselves? This is disgusting! It wouldn't be so bad if these towels belonged to my rich and handsome husband." She laughed and then added playfully, "Maybe in a few years." She then said, "I was born to be the wife of a prominent politician or doctor or professional athlete. You all can be career women if you want to. I want financial security."

"What about love?" questioned Charlotte.

"That would be nice too, but not a necessity," answered Vivian.

"Vivian!" the others shouted in unison.

Vivian just laughed.

Each of the four young women was prepared for the world of work in distinctly different career fields: nursing for Charlotte, business for Vivian, education for Florence, and Stella—well, Stella chose the theater by way of professional English and was headed for California, determined to become a national sensation on the big screen. She had no relatives in California and, except for a so-called talent agent she met six months ago through a magazine ad, did not know anyone west of the Mississippi River. However, if anyone could break into Hollywood, Stella was sure it would be her.

Cap, gown, black shoes, black dress, and those signature pearls—everything was in order for the graduation ceremony.

No one remembered the speaker or the eloquent words of wisdom that were spoken. The only thing that rushed to the front of the girls' minds was the trepidation that comes from leaving the safe, extended adolescence sphere of college life for the unpredictable and often-scary world of work.

After the official ceremonies were over, each graduate joined their respective family and friends, who helped them load trunks, boxes, and suitcases with all the things they acquired during the four years of their undergraduate experience and took them back home.

Charlotte was assisted by her mother, Rose, and her sister Barbara. Her mother was complaining about the amount of stuff Charlotte had accumulated over the past four years, and Barbara was quizzing Charlotte on when she would be moving out from Mom's and if she had a job lined up.

Florence was pleasantly surprised when she found out the day before that her mother, Eleanor, and two of her siblings, Roberta and Geraldine, were coming to her college graduation and would be helping her pack to move back. They seemed genuinely proud of Florence and happy to have at least one family member graduate from college. It was the first time her mother and sisters had been on a college campus, and they were almost mesmerized by the number of cute boys they saw.

Stella managed to gather up the contents of her dorm room in record time, and as soon as the ceremony was over, she would head west to make her fortune in Hollywood, California. As she was saying her goodbyes to the many friends she had made, she would discretely look over her shoulder to search the crowd for any evidence of a family member. Not finding any, she flashed that gorgeous smile of hers to all she met and continued dispensing hugs and best wishes to everyone she knew.

Vivian, along with her mother Marianne; and her Aunt Ruby helped get her things packed and loaded in the car. There would not have been enough room in Marianne's car for all of Vivian's belongings had it not been for the fact that she had already shipped one trunk home.

The four girls came to campus as slightly naive, immature, and inexperienced individuals, but after growing personally, socially, and intellectually, they were leaving as confident, self-assured young women who were ready to take their places in society. Before they departed, they hugged, cried, and said their goodbyes and promised emphatically to keep in touch.

CHAPTER 3

Meet Vivian

THE BABY WAS homeless from birth and didn't even have a name. Within hours of delivery, her mother slipped out, abandoning her to the care of the hospital staff. She was given the name Marianne Martin and placed in the foster-care system. Marianne was moved from one foster home to another and often went to bed at night unsure where she would be the next day. Some of the foster homes were traumatic for Marianne, so she learned to cope by pretending she was one of the characters she met through a book of fairy tales that she received one Christmas from a local charity. She especially liked the ones where everyone lived happily ever after. That's what she was praying for—a "happily ever after" life. Once she aged out of foster care, she was on her own. Had it not been for her best friend, Ruby Jones, she would have been homeless. Ruby convinced her mother to let Marianne live with them until she saved enough money to get her own apartment. After just four months, Marianne had saved enough to move into a place of her own. For the first time in her life, she knew where she would be the next day.

Marianne started dating a guy that she met at church—Henry John Anderson; everyone called him Henry John. He was older than Marianne by seven years, was recently divorced, and was living with his brother in the apartment across the street from her. Henry John had a steady job at the local mill and had a car of his own. They had been dating for six months when Henry John asked Marianne to marry him, and she said yes. Incidentally, Henry John's brother was also getting married and moving across town with his new wife. Marianne and Henry John said their vows before a justice of the peace, Ruby standing up for them. They moved into Marianne's apartment, and all seemed to

---

go well. Marianne worked as a maid and a cook for a well-to-do family and was able to use her salary to turn her little apartment into a home.

Eighteen months into the marriage, Marianne had great news to share with her husband. She cooked his favorite dinner of southern pot roast with garden-root vegetables and angel biscuits. A belly full of her pot roast and biscuits always put Henry John in a good mood. She learned to make biscuits while living in foster care at the Lindseys'. There were five other foster children in the home, and Marianne's job was to make bread for every meal. This skill came in handy for a young bride with a hungry husband.

Henry John came home later than usual that night, and when he opened the door, he was not in a good mood. He smelled of alcohol—a lot of alcohol. Marianne suspected that Henry John was drinking more often, and she was more than a little concerned. As soon as he sat down at the table, Marianne announced with excitement that they were going to have a baby.

Instead of sharing her enthusiasm, Henry John hit the ceiling. Marianne had never seen this side of him before. It was like he went into a rage. He said they didn't need another mouth to feed. He told Marianne that he had been let go from his job three days ago and didn't have any money for a baby. Marianne tried to console him, assuring him that they could make it on her salary for a few weeks until he got another job.

But it didn't work out the way she envisioned. Henry John looked for work for about two weeks, but then he just stopped looking. He would be in bed when Marianne went to work and still be there when she got back. Then he started leaving the house after supper, begging for and then demanding money from Marianne. He would not come back until the wee hours of the morning, explaining that he was at his brother's house playing cards, trying to win her some money.

As Marianne got bigger and bigger, Henry John got drunker and drunker. When Marianne went to the hospital to deliver little Vivian Joyce, Henry John appeared to get himself together and seemed to actually fall in love with the baby. He finally found a job, and things were looking up. But within six weeks, Henry John lost his job again.

This time, he was fired for drinking on the job. When he finally came home that night, he was in an angry mood. He started directing his frustration and anger toward Marianne and even toward the baby. Little Vivian developed colic and cried almost nonstop. This would set Henry John off, and he would explode in a fit of agitation and anger. He expressed his anger first through verbal abuse, but things soon turned physical. Their neighbors had called and asked the police several times to investigate the noises coming from their apartment but they knew instinctively what was happening. But every time Marianne would come up with one excuse after another and not press charges.

By the time Vivian was six months old, Marianne had become an expert at hiding bruises and black eyes. But tonight was different. Henry John went after her baby, yelling at little Vivian Joyce to shut up or she would get the same thing her mother got. Marianne had had enough. She realized the time to make a move was now because she had to protect her child. As soon as Henry John went to sleep in a drunken stupor, Marianne quickly called the police and told them about how abusive Henry John was and that she was afraid for her life and the life of her baby. When she hung up the telephone, she heard Henry John waking up, and although it was snowing, she decided to make a run for it, knowing that the police were on the way. She quickly grabbed her hat and coat, wrapped the baby in two heavy blankets, and sneaked out the door, forgetting that she only had on bedroom shoes. She ran straight for the woods behind the apartment complex. She hid there with no food or water, nursing a six-month-old all night until she was sure Henry John was arrested. Marianne made it through the night by going into survivor mode, pretending she was the miller's daughter and trying to save her baby from Rumpelstiltskin, Henry John being Rumpelstiltskin.

After Henry John was arrested, Marianne testified of the abuse she suffered at his hand. At the trial, she found out he had numerous abuse and assault charges—some from his first wife and some from places of employment from which he had been fired. She also found out that he had not paid the rent on their apartment for four months, their bank accounts were overdrawn, and the car Marianne was driving was being repossessed because her husband had taken the money she gave him for car payments and gambled it away. The landlord informed her that she had seven days to vacate her apartment.

It was difficult to find suitable housing with her salary and still have something left for her baby. Marianne had not found anywhere to move by the time the sheriff came to evict her. Having little options, she had to take charity anywhere she could find it. But she was too proud to admit she was penniless and convinced those around her and herself that she was waiting for her security deposit so she could get another apartment. The money was being held up because of Henry John. She just needed to find somewhere to stay for a few weeks until the check cleared. When she found someone willing to take her and her daughter in, she insisted that it would only be for a few weeks.

She stayed with Floyd and Rachael Holly for three months until Floyd started making unwelcome advances at Marianne and Rachael asked her to leave. She was homeless until Pastor Higgins and his wife took them in. They spent eighteen months in the parsonage with them until their son Jack moved back in with his children after his wife left him.

They were homeless again.

They lived with her friend Judith for three years until she decided to get married and move to Tennessee. She would be leaving in two months.

Marianne and her child would be homeless once more.

Aunt Ruby found out that Marianne and little Vivian Joyce would have no place to stay after Judith moved with her new husband, so she opened her house to them. Aunt Ruby was not really Vivian's aunt. Marianne and Ruby had been best friends since high school, but over the years, Ruby Jones had become known as Aunt Ruby to everyone in the small South Carolina community. It was probably because she never married and had no children of her own and because her house was a safe place where no one was ever turned away. Every hungry child knew they could get a sandwich from Aunt Ruby, no questions asked. She was the one you went to for that cup of sugar or extra pair of stockings or bail money, and no one but the two of you would ever know. She spoke her mind and always told the truth, and although she stood only four feet eleven, she didn't back down from anyone, be he a sheriff or a preacher.

When Aunt Ruby took them in, Marianne and little Vivian Joyce felt they had finally found a permanent home.

But after approximately five years of stability, Aunt Ruby pulled Marianne aside and announced with restrained excitement that she would be leaving South Carolina in two weeks to move to Pennsylvania with her older brother who had found her a job in the factory where he worked. Unfortunately, Marianne and her daughter could not remain in the house because it belonged to her brother and he was selling it.

Homeless. Again.

"Why don't you come to Philadelphia with me, Marianne? You and Vivian Joyce," Aunt Ruby offered. "You know there is nothing here for you, and Henry John will be getting out of jail in six months, and you know you need to be gone when he gets out because he will come looking for you and Vivian Joyce," warned Aunt Ruby.

Marianne realized that Ruby was right. She also knew that she had just about exhausted the list of people in town who would be willing to take her and her nine-year-old in. Facing reality, Marianne thanked Ruby and said she and her daughter would move with her to Philadelphia only if she would let her pay for all the train tickets.

Marianne sold everything she could not carry in two boxes, purchased the train tickets to Philadelphia, and told Vivian Joyce that they were going on a great vacation. With Vivian Joyce in tow, along with the two boxes that held all their possessions, Marianne left the South behind. She didn't know what the future would bring, but she knew it had to be better than the past.

Ruby's brother Willis arranged for Ruby, Marianne, and Vivian Joyce to stay at his house, although they had to share one bedroom with Marianne and her daughter sleeping on the floor. Vivian Joyce had picked up her mother's coping mechanism and pretended they were camping out. Marianne was offered a job at the factory along with Ruby but did not make it through the training because the job required standing for long periods of time. Since Marianne had acquired a bad case of frostbite arthritis in her feet from that winter night that she spent in the woods wearing only bedroom shoes while running from Henry John, she could not stand in one place for too long. Marianne decided to look for a different type of job that didn't require long-term standing. Her strengths were cooking, cleaning, and housekeeping. Ruby suggested that Marianne look for domestic-worker positions, which were always in demand on the other side of the tracks. So the following morning, Marianne put on her best church dress and hat and made sure Vivian was dressed as cute as possible with hair ribbons, and they caught the bus headed for the other side of town. When they got off the bus, Vivian thought she was in another city. She had never seen such large and beautiful houses. The place was like something out of one of the fairy tales her mother read to her at night. Vivian felt like this was where she belonged, like a princess coming home. Her mother taught her how to act around people who had what she needed—not manipulation, just survival. She was polite, attentive, and complimentary and knew that children should speak only when spoken to. Marianne Anderson applied for a domestic position in the home of Mr. and Mrs. George and Harriett Fitzgerald—prominent, childless middle-aged socialites. George Fitzgerald was a retired surgeon. He had a stroke two years ago, was practically bedridden, and had a private nurse who attended to him daily. Harriett Fitzgerald was a retired concert pianist who was recently sidelined by arthritis in her left hand. She was impressed that Marianne was from the South as she was. She thought southerners were born knowing how to keep house and cook. She was pleased that Marianne had a daughter and took a liking to the sweet and gentle disposition that Vivian Joyce exhibited as she quietly sat by her mother. Harriett's daughter, Portia, had died from rheumatic fever when she was just fifteen years old, and nothing had filled her house or her heart like the presence of a child. By the time the interview was over, Marianne had secured a live-in position for her sake and Vivian Joyce's. Marianne would do all the major cleaning, mop the floors, change the bed linens, and cook, and her daughter would do the laundry and the ironing. Mrs. Fitzgerald would be getting two employees for the price of one.

Marianne and her daughter moved into the housekeeping quarters, complete with two beds and a separate bathroom. Vivian Joyce caught on to doing the laundry and ironing quickly. She loved the elegance of Mrs. Fitzgerald's house, especially her baby grand piano and sparkling chandeliers. She pretended the house belonged to her and her mother and Mrs. Fitzgerald was their fairy godmother. She looked forward to the times when Mrs. Fitzgerald would invite her to sit quietly as she played the piano. But what Vivian Joyce enjoyed most of all was running errands with her mother, especially grocery shopping. Once a week, Mrs. Fitzgerald would let Marianne drive her black 1962 Cadillac Coupe De Ville—a two-door hardtop—to get groceries. When they would pull up to the store, Vivian Joyce would get out of the car like Cinderella stepping out of her carriage.

Vivian practically grew up in the Fitzgerald house. Four years after they moved in, Mr. Fitzgerald died. She and her mother became traveling companions for Mrs. Fitzgerald and often accompanied her to Myrtle Beach, South Carolina, in the summer and Nantucket, Massachusetts, in the fall. Six months before Vivian graduated from high school, Harriett Fitzgerald died. Marianne and Vivian had to move, but this time, to their surprise, Mrs. Fitzgerald's will provided Marianne with enough money to purchase a very modest house and included a clause that fully funded Vivian's college education. Mrs. Fitzgerald *was* their fairy godmother.

CHAPTER 4

Meet Stella

S TELLA WAS BORN Estella Louisa Miller in Philadelphia, Pennsylvania, into a working-class family; it was composed of a mother, a father, and three girls. Her father, Frank, was a long-distance truck driver, although Stella never saw a truck in the driveway. Her mother, Jean, worked as a file clerk at a retirement home. Stella's two older sisters, Francis and Johnnie Mae, were two and four years her senior, respectively. Somewhat skinny and tall for her age, Stella was a naturally cute child with a beautiful smile, a quick wit, and a warm demeanor. People fell in love with her almost immediately. It was not so for Francis and Johnnie Mae. They were pretty enough but did not have inviting personalities. Jean never denied Francis or Johnnie Mae any small treasure, but her generosity was withheld from Stella with the excuse that she was too young and her day would come. Discards and hand-me-downs from her sisters found their way to Stella, who was always appreciative because of the love she had for them.

The family always seemed to be living paycheck to paycheck, which was often the subject of much yelling and fighting between Jean and Frank. Jean would accuse Frank of not bringing home enough money, and Frank's complaint always ended with the phrase "extra mouth to feed."

On one particularly cold and wet Philadelphia afternoon, two days after Stella's sixteenth birthday, Jean and Frank were having one of their usual fights; this one was particularly loud. Stella and her sisters continued their breakfast, oblivious to the usual noise coming from their parents' bedroom. The fight seemed to last much longer than usual, and this time, it ended with Frank storming out, suitcase in hand, his head narrowly missing contact with the flower vase Jean threw in his direction.

Jean stayed in her room for two days, forbidding anyone to make any noise. Francis and Johnnie Mae dismissed Jean's command and carried on as usual, but Stella complied as best she could. At the sound of any noise, Jean would rush out of her room and demand to know who was causing the disturbance. Francis and Johnnie Mae conspired and accused Stella as usual. Jean characteristically took their word, and this morning, she warned Stella that if she couldn't obey, she would have to leave the house as well.

"Leave and go where, Mother?" answered Stella sarcastically.

"And stop calling me 'Mother'! I am not your mother!" shouted Jean. "I am your aunt!"

"Mother, are you crazy?" asked Francis.

"Are you trying to say you and Daddy are not our parents?" laughed Johnnie Mae.

"I am *your* mother, Johnnie Mae—yours and Francis's. Just not Stella's," said Jean, her voice becoming a little subdued, which let the girls know she was serious.

She turned to Stella and continued, "I should have told you long before now."

"Mother, I don't understand. Are you for real?" questioned Stella.

"Sit down, Stella."

She continued, "I should have told you earlier, but I adopted you after Grace, your mother and my older sister, died in a train wreck. She was on her way back home from some college in Europe somewhere. She flew back to Washington, DC, and caught the train to Philadelphia, but ten miles outside of Baltimore, the train jumped the tracks. Five people were killed, including Grace. No one knew at the time that Grace was bringing back with her a sixth-month-old baby—you—who survived the train crash without a scratch. With no other relatives, they contacted me, and that's how you came to live with me."

Jean turned to Francis. "Francis, you and Johnnie Mae were babies yourselves—you only four years old and Johnnie May about eighteen months. You both just thought I went to the hospital and brought back a new baby."

"So that's why Stella got that white streak in her hair and we don't", observed Francis.

Stella's reality was turned upside down, and her mind went blank for a few minutes. Jean was still talking, but Stella could not absorb another word. It was like someone trying to make a teacup hold a river of water, and she was emotionally drowning.

Why Jean chose this day to turn Stella's world upside down, she never learned. Maybe it was because Frank left. Or maybe it was because she lost her job at the retirement home or she never got over the fact that Grace left her. Whatever the reason, Jean chose this time to rid herself of the obvious burden of caring for someone else's child.

Without missing a beat, Jean continued, "Now that you know, Stella, it's time for you to start pulling your weight around here. I have taken care of you these sixteen years, getting nothing for my trouble. I can't afford to continue to feed an extra mouth."

"Extra mouth"—there it was again. Stella realized she was not family—just an extra mouth.

Johnnie Mae seemed just as stunned and upset as Stella, but Francis dismissed it as nothing earthshaking.

That was the first day Stella felt like the orphan she was.

Jean became more distant as the days went by, seemingly thinking she was justified to blame Stella for Frank's leaving and for everything else that went wrong. Stella found a job at a local grocery store after school and gave Jean her paycheck each week. She became invisible at home, losing herself in her schoolwork. Francis and Johnnie Mae, although older than Stella, were not required to work. They spent their days shopping and their nights partying. Stella had no money left after paying Jean for her upkeep, so she continued receiving hand-me-downs from Francis and Johnnie Mae.

She didn't mind wearing old clothes in elementary and junior high because she thought they were from sisters who loved her, but high school was another matter. She determined that if she had to wear their hand-me-downs, they would not look like such. Stella became an expert at adding lace to the bottoms or tops of dresses, replacing missing buttons with unique ones, and even dying old clothes a different color. She became so creative that her friends began to notice her style and started going to her for fashion advice. By the eleventh grade, she had won two fashion-design contests, and in her senior year, she received the prestigious J. Clara Fashion Innovations Award, which came with a modest scholarship to attend any college of her choice.

Stella was an excellent student and realized that college was her ticket out of Aunt Jean's house. After her high school graduation was over, and as soon as she could, Stella packed her bags and left for college, determined to get as far away from her loneliness as she could and find her place in life. Jean was not anxious for Stella to leave because it meant that she would not be getting any more money from Stella, but at least the extra mouth would be gone.

CHAPTER 5

Meet Florence

E LEANOR SPENCER HAD been a popular teenager in high school and cultivated that popularity throughout young adulthood. She was attractive and a social butterfly and lived for compliments from all the men—young and old and single and married alike. She saw no problem in dating several men at the same time and often played one against another. By the time she was nineteen, she was an unwed mother of two and had unknowingly earned the reputation of a "garden tool every man used but didn't want to own." It did not take her long to go through most of the men in town.

The community was abuzz with news of a new unmarried pastor coming to town. All the single women prepared to compete for the affections of the young Reverend Eric Robinson. Eleanor thought she would also throw her hat in the ring and showed up at church on the first Sunday Rev. Robinson arrived. After the service, the mothers' board prepared a repast to welcome the new pastor. As soon as the church women saw Eleanor walking in while wearing alluring attire, they immediately sprang into action to circumvent any contact between the new reverend and Eleanor. What the church women were up to became evident to Eleanor, but she actually seemed surprised when she overheard one of them say something about an unwed woman being unfit for decent men.

Societal and religious forces began to press upon Eleanor the need to find a husband. She decided to see if there were any single men in the church who could help her gain some sense of respectability. Eleanor settled on George Spencer; he was somewhat dim-witted, but he was a faithful member of the church and a deacon, and marrying him would certainly elevate her standing among the congregation. Within three months, Eleanor had tied the knot with Deacon George, a handyman that everyone in the community loved. Eleanor had a big wedding and invited every Tom, Dick, and Harry. She wanted the whole town to know that she was fit company now because she was the wife of a church deacon.

Shortly after the wedding, Eleanor stopped displaying any sign of love or affection toward George—not only in her touch but also in her tone of voice. It was rumored that she never really stopped sleeping around. Within two years of marriage, Eleanor was pregnant. This new baby was a boy and looked remarkably like his two sisters. Her neighbor Ralph Milton, who was also a deacon in the church, was rumored to be this baby's daddy also. The short bowed legs were the giveaway. George proudly paraded this baby at church but was oblivious to the gossip that was going on behind his back. But Eleanor was thrilled that she had a son. It was interesting that she did not name him George Jr. but named the baby after her father, Jacob. A year later, Eleanor was pregnant again, but unlike her other three pregnancies, she had a difficult time. She was sick almost the entire nine months and had to endure over twenty-four hours of labor. It was a girl.

This baby was different. She was longer than the others with unusually big eyes. They were not only big but also brown, not light gray like her siblings'. And she had jet-black hair—lots of it. Even before her mother brought her home from the hospital, the gossip had started. Who was this baby's daddy? She certainly didn't have the same father as the first three.

George asked Eleanor to name the baby after his mother, Florence. Eleanor appeared indifferent. She did not seem to be as pleased with the birth of little Florence as she had been with Jacob's. As Florence grew, it became evident that this child certainly was not Ralph's. The other three children were lazy and indifferent, lacked ambition, and showed little interest in the world around them. Florence was just the opposite. She was cute, sweet, a little loud for a child her age, very confident and self-assured, curious, and smart as a whip—no bowed legs, either. At six years old, she knew more than all her siblings combined, and even the neighborhood children sought her out for help with homework.

If not Ralph, then who? Maybe George Spencer was this baby's daddy. She did have his eyes, and he absolutely adored her. He constantly bragged about her to anyone who would listen.

Eleanor was just the opposite. She seemed to almost resent Florence. She complained about her hair, her height, her voice—everything. Eleanor insisted that Florence do most of the chores even though she was the youngest because she was quick and accurate but never, ever gave her credit for anything she did well. This attitude was adopted by her siblings. Everything that went wrong was Florence's fault.

But oh, how George loved her. He never came home without something special for Florence—a new dress or trinket or candy—and this elicited additional dislike from Eleanor and the other children. Maybe he wasn't as dim-witted as people thought he was and instinctively knew that Florence was his only child.

Florence and her father formed a special bond. They liked the same things: church, lemonade, hot dogs, football, and fishing—in that order. No one else in the family shared their passions. Florence learned to enjoy sports at the same high volume as George and his friends, although George was as uncoordinated as a bull in a china shop. But this was not so for Florence. She was a great ball handler and could throw, shoot, and dribble with the best of them. She even had a jock's mouth, which she learned at her father's knee and he never corrected her. Often she was the only girl watching with the men because she was an expert at calling the plays and at remembering the vital statistics of any team. Once they started watching sports, Eleanor used it as an excuse to leave the house and not return until the wee hours of the morning.

One afternoon, Florence brought her father a lemonade and a hot dog and went back in the kitchen to fix a hot dog for herself. When she returned, she noticed that he had not taken a bite. She called out to her father, and he did not answer. George had died suddenly from an apparent heart attack.

The days that followed George's death were a bit of a blur for Florence. She remembered an insurance agent coming to the house to discuss George's life-insurance payout. Eleanor told the family that her husband had taken out a small life-insurance policy, and she decided to spend the proceeds on a respectable funeral for him. And what a funeral it was. Eleanor was always chasing a reputation of good social standing, but it always eluded her due to her own actions. For instance, a year after she married George, she was caught in the choir loft in the arms of Ralph Milton, the same Ralph who was rumored to be the father of three of her four children. She thought that if she spared no expense on George's funeral, the community would forget about her infidelity and be convinced that she really did love her husband.

Eleanor did not use the local undertaker but went twenty-five miles away to employ the services of Thompson Funeral and Cremation Services. Everyone knew they were the most expensive and generally catered to the elite of the county. Eleanor paid for extravagances such as a stretch white-and-gold limousine, a designer casket, two hundred embossed programs in full color with more glamour pictures of herself than George, a jazz band, the releasing of doves at the cemetery, and a catered sit-down repast. She acted the part of the grieving widow, although George and Eleanor were only roommates for the last 10 years of their marriage. But she wanted to be the center of attention and played the widow card for all it was worth. She made sure that everyone would talk about the fancy funeral that Eleanor Anderson had for her loving husband, Deacon George, for years to come.

After the funeral, Florence realized that the one person in her life that she could always depend on was gone. She needed to find a place of refuge to get away from the coldness of her mother and siblings, and she found it at school and at church.

Florence enjoyed everything at school. The chess club as well as the debate club elected her president. By her senior year, she was the captain of the girls' basketball team, a member of the softball team, and a member of the chorus. Florence's free time was devoted to church activities—youth choir, junior ushers, and youth outreach. Florence was the president of the mass choir and a state representative at the church's national convention. In spite of all her accomplishments, she seldom received any encouragement or praise from her family.

None of her siblings shared Florence's interest in school or church. They spent their time moving from one temporary job to another, earning just enough money to keep them supplied with cigarettes and beer. They all still lived at home, and Eleanor was happy to have them there. Florence continued doing most of the chores—the laundry, cooking, and dishwashing—and she still contributed her share of the living expenses with the earnings from her part-time tutoring job. In spite of her family's indifference to her, Florence loved them.

With her father gone, Florence thought that her dream of going to college was dead as well. She knew she couldn't ask her mother for any money. But one day after church, as she was hanging up the choir robes, she overheard Harry Smith, a bank manager, saying something to Pastor Robinson about George taking out insurance so Florence could go to college. When Florence asked her mother about the conversation, Eleanor almost hit the roof and told her that funerals were very expensive, and since she wanted George to have a proper burial, she spent almost all the life-insurance money on his funeral. She kept just a little to help around the house.

Florence was not aware at the time, but soon found out that she had qualified for several scholarships, including the one from the local lodge where George had been a faithful member. When she told her mother that she had enough money for college, Eleanor seemed almost pleased. She told Florence that she couldn't drive her to the college, but as a graduation present, she would buy her a one-way bus ticket there. After Florence packed her belongings, said goodbye to her family and all her friends at church, and thanked Rev. Robinson for his support over the years, she boarded the bus with her belongings and headed for college and a new life.

CHAPTER 6

Meet Charlotte

CHARLOTTE TIMMONS NEVER had a care in the world when she was a child. She was the younger of two girls of a family with a wonderful stay-at-home mother and a strong father. Born during the post–World War II baby boom, Charlotte's childhood was one of comfort and security. Her father worked for a local electrical company, and her mother was always a homemaker. Charlotte's family was more financially stable than most of the families on her street. Their house was modest but immaculate, the girls were neatly dressed and well-behaved, and the yard was consistently well-groomed.

As their neighbors passed the Timmons' house, they would be rewarded with the mouthwatering aroma of something being freshly baked. They could be seen turning their heads, lifting their noses, and smiling while whispering, "Something sure smells good!"

When Charlotte was in junior high school, her father reenlisted in the military after having been honorably discharged eight years earlier. He reenlisted because the company he was working for had gone out of business. He had been trained as an electrician while he was working in the engine room of an attack-transport vessel during his initial enlistment, and such a skill was always in demand in the military. When Charlotte found out that her father was going overseas, she cried, thinking he was never coming back. He did, but he was not home for long because he was deployed again and again. Charlotte had always been a daddy's girl, and every time her father was home on leave, she wanted him to spend all his time with her. She even resented the times when her mother wanted him all to herself.

"Wake up, Charlotte."

Half-asleep, Charlotte mumbled something under her breath and thought she was dreaming until she was shaken awake by her older sister, Barbara.

"Why did you wake me up? What's going on?"

"Charlotte, be quiet and come with me. Mom wants us downstairs—now!"

Barbara led her to the top of the stairs. They heard the muffled voice of one of two uniformed men standing in their living room. From their appearance, Charlotte deduced that they were military police. They were talking with their mother in a quiet and reserved tone, and Charlotte could make out only a few words: "entrusted me," "deep regret," "husband," "death notification," and "chaplain." Then a most mournful cry went forth from their mother, and she seemed to fall into the arms of one of the uniformed men.

"Mother! Mother! What's wrong?" said Barbara as she ran to their mother. Charlotte just stood at the top of the stairs, not wanting to hear anything else. This one moment changed their family trajectory for all time.

Charlotte's father was away on his second tour of duty in Vietnam and was scheduled to return in three weeks. He made it home but not in the way he or his family imagined.

Charlotte was distraught over the death of her father. She could not imagine that anyone else loved him and missed him as much as she did. But as she watched her mother Rose go through the funeral with such an air of grace and sophistication, Charlotte almost forgot to grieve. Rose was determined to give her husband the most dignified homegoing—one that befitted the husband, father, and war hero that Sergeant Nebraska McDaniel Timmons was.

After the services were finally over and Rose Timmons was satisfied that she had given her husband a proper funeral and had appropriately and eloquently thanked everyone who had tried to comfort her and her family during their hour of need, the air just seemed to go out of her. She became withdrawn, despondent, and reclusive. She neglected the house and even herself. She stayed in bed most of the day and began to drink heavily—this from a woman who thought drinking wine at Thanksgiving was a mortal sin. Charlotte and Barbara stayed as close to their mother as possible, but Barbara had to return to college, and Charlotte drowned herself in senior high activities, leaving Rose with even more time on her hands to wallow in self-pity. She became stagnant; she was stuck in a bubble of grief and was dying.

Providence seemed to step in at the right time. Grandma Beulah, Rose's mother-in-law, fell in a bathroom and broke her hip. This near tragedy ironically became her mother's life preserver. Since Nebraska was Grandma Beulah's only child, Rose invited her to come live with her after she got out of rehab. This gave Rose a reason for living. She had someone who needed her again.

For the first time in her life, Charlotte was able to spend quality time with her grandmother. She had no idea that her grandmother had lived such as colorful life. And now at ninety-two, Grandma Beulah opened her treasure chest of memories and eagerly shared them with Charlotte. She came from a family of seven siblings (all of which preceded her in death), owned her own bakery (which employed ten people), was the first person in her small town to travel out of the country, and became a single mother at thirty-two just because she wanted to, but she never married. Charlotte asked her why she never married, and Grandma Beulah told her it was because she never met a man as handsome as her father or as smart as she was. She always had a saying for practically every situation, such as "Every shut eye ain't sleep," "You can get a man to do anything for you if you let him think it's his idea," "You can catch more flies with honey than with vinegar," "Don't count your chickens before they are hatched," "Don't start anything you don't want to finish," and other life lessons. After all, Grandma Beulah had outlived everyone she knew.

Upon her high school graduation, Charlotte decided to go to college and become a nurse. The experience of helping her mother care for Grandma Beulah helped her make that decision.

CHAPTER 7

A Character Molding Experience

CHARLOTTE, STELLA, FLORENCE, and Vivian arrived at college during a time when the social fabric of the country was saturated with political activism as evidenced by the number of nonviolent demonstrations and protests that occurred. The college experience provides the avenue to transition from a dependent teenager into an independent adult. Each of the four freshmen brought with her baggage from her childhood that influenced how she embraced college life in her own unique way.

Charlotte

Charlotte suggested to her mother Rose that if she did not feel well, she did not have to go to the campus with her on move-in day. It was only six months ago that Grandma Beulah died, and Rose had cared for her until the end. Rose herself suffered from emphysema and had been experiencing breathing problems for the past week. But she insisted that she would have it no other way; she would accompany her youngest daughter to college just as she did for her older daughter. She felt it was her duty to help Charlotte decorate her dormitory room and meet her roommates. Rose also wanted to take one last opportunity to impart some motherly wisdom to Charlotte. Rose had always been a great and caring mother who took her role seriously. Sprinkled among the dos and don'ts, Rose admonished Charlotte to do the following:

"Try new things—within reason—as long as it is not immoral, illegal, or fattening. Eat properly, get enough sleep, and don't forget to call home once a week."

After her mother concluded her advice, she went down the hall to investigate who the other students were that would be living in the same dormitory as her little girl. Barbara pulled Charlotte aside to give her the most important and valuable advice that only a big sister who had just graduated from college could give: a lesson on understanding college men.

"As a freshman, take this year to investigate all the boys. Do not miss class, go to every athletic game, attend every concert, never miss a symposium, and investigate every cause, and once you see some boys you like, only double-date. All the guys are strangers and many are potential users and abusers, mama boys, jocks, pretty boys, and nerds.

"As a sophomore, go to the library, go to tutoring, become involved with the student government, and join clubs such as the debate club, the political-action club, and the entrepreneurial club. Check out the guys that you see there because they will have potential.

"As a junior, you should have narrowed the field down to two or three guys with whom you have something in common.

"As a senior, you should have found someone who would be a good prospect for a husband—if you are looking for one. Remember, college is the last place where you will have access to so many eligible men in one place. Once you graduate, the odds are no longer in your favor. If you want a husband, this is the best place to find one. That's how I made sure Philip found me."

Barbara ended her speech with a wink and a smile.

And with that, Rose and Barbara left Charlotte standing on the steps of the honors dorm and waving goodbye. Charlotte went back to her room, sat down at her desk, and started writing out her action plan for the first week. *Lesson One: Don't miss class.* Organization and order were Charlotte's constant companions.

When her roommate finally arrived the next day, Charlotte immediately knew that they would get along very well. Aisha Mitchell was friendly, bubbly, and full of life. She drove herself to the college in a new car that her parents bought her for her high school graduation. She was independent, already engaged to her high school sweetheart, and was absolutely in love. She had been a cheerleader in high school just like Charlotte, and both would be auditioning for the cheering squad. Aisha admitted to Charlotte that she probably would not be around much because her fiancé was also a freshman at the college and they would be spending a lot of time together.

Florence

Florence took the Greyhound bus from her hometown to the college. She had never ventured over thirty miles from home except when she went to church conferences, and those had chaperones. Florence was somewhat overwhelmed when she saw the college and the surrounding city for the first time. She was impressed by the designs of the campus buildings and the friendliness of the students and staff. She located the honors dorm, got her room key, and settled in. She unpacked her one suitcase, hung up her one coat, and placed her one photograph of her father, George, on her desk and waited for the arrival of her roommate.

An hour later, Victoria Vanstory of Texas, her new roommate, arrived. She was accompanied by her mother, two sisters, and aunt. After the introductions, Victoria's mother looked around the room and said, "Florence, dear, I know this is not all you have. When will you be moving the rest of your things in?"

Knowing what she meant, Florence sarcastically but politely replied, "Thank you so much for noticing that I am thrifty with the fortune my parents left for me. And if you will excuse me, I will give you room to unpack."

And with that, Florence left the room.

When she returned, she almost threw up. The room was decorated in everything pink. Rug, lamp, upholstered desk chair, alarm clock, wall calendar—everything was pink. Victoria was friendly enough, but Florence was not a fan of the color pink. It appeared that she was also financially secure. Florence got to college on scholarships and nothing more. It was apparent that Victoria was there to get a husband, based on the amount of perfumes and makeup that lined her dresser, while Florence was there to get a life. The one thing they silently agreed on was that as roommates, they were not a good fit, but they determined to tolerate each other for now. Besides, Victoria confessed, she was on a mission to find a husband and would be gone by her sophomore year. Victoria indeed found that husband, and after her freshman year, she did not return, leaving room for Florence to find another roommate.

Stella

Being accepted into college proved to be a means of escape for Stella. Her only stumbling block was affording the tuition. She received no help from her family, and she realized that the scholarship she received would only pay for two-thirds of her fees. So during the summer after her high school graduation, Stella worked several jobs. Along with clerking at the grocery store full-time, she took part-time jobs at the drugstore and the laundromat and even cleaned houses. No job was beneath her. By the end of summer, Stella had actually made enough money for the first semester's tuition, but Jean insisted that she pay her for room and board in advance. After satisfying Jean, Stella had only $250 left. This was nowhere near enough to cover the balance of her tuition for the fall semester. When Stella told Jean that she didn't have enough money left to go back to school, Jean almost seemed happy.

"Well, what do you expect me to do? You are just like your mother. You need to forget about college and get a real job. I think they are hiring at the bakery," offered Jean.

Stella reluctantly contacted the registrar at the college to inform him that she would not be able to attend the fall semester because she had only been able to save $250, but she asked him to hold her spot for the spring. One week later, Stella received a certified letter from the college registrar that invited her to come and bring whatever she had and told her the college would help make up the difference with grants and student employment. Stella couldn't believe it. She was so unspeakably grateful but decided not to tell Jean immediately. Stella waited until the day before she was to leave to tell Jean that the college found her a job in the library to help with her tuition so she would be leaving after all.

The transition from high school to college is not always a smooth one, but it proved to be a liberating and eye-opening experience for Stella. When she arrived on campus and checked into her dormitory room, she felt like she had come home. Since she arrived before her roommate, she chose her side of the room, unpacked her bags, and began to reflect on her life. She had not taken time before to fully process the fact that Jean was not her mother and that Francis and Johnnie Mae were not really her sisters. Now she understood why she never really had that mother-daughter bond with Jean and always felt that something was missing in their relationship. Jean never hugged her or spoke loving words to her as she had heard her talking to Francis and Johnnie Mae. She never remembered sitting on Jean's lap or even holding her hand. All Stella wanted was a mother's love. She accepted the fact that to Jean, she had always been just another mouth to feed. She felt alone.

Fortunately, she had only a few hours to feel that way because in no time at all, she heard someone outside her door. That someone said, "Mommy, I think this is Room 244."

Vivian

Vivian arrived at the college in a classic black Cadillac that was driven by her mother, Marianne, which gave the impression that she was some celebrity or someone from a wealthy family. She brought with her four suitcases filled with the latest fashions that Mrs. Fitzgerald, her benefactor, insisted on buying for her some time ago. Vivian graduated at the top of her class and from one of the most prestigious private high schools in Philadelphia, thanks to her fairy godmother.

Vivian sailed into the room, smiling like a Scarlett O'Hara wannabe, and was accompanied by two women—one of which, Stella assumed, was her mother—and a dog so small that Stella thought it was a rat. Before Stella could escape, "Ms. Scarlett" immediately reached out and hugged her. She kissed Stella on each cheek like they were old friends and announced in the fakest southern drawl that she was Ms. Vivian Miller Anderson, her new roomie. She introduced one of the women with her as her mommy, Mrs. Marianne Miller Anderson, and introduced the other one as her Auntie Ruby. Stella made polite conversation, excused herself as fast as she could so that Ms. Vivian Miller Anderson could get unpacked, and say goodbye to her entourage.

Stella decided to give this pretentious, pompous, and ostentatious person the benefit of the doubt. Once Stella got to know Vivian, to her surprise, she began to really like her. She proved to be decent company. They both had good study habits, liked their music loud, and respected each other's privacy when they had "men on the hall." Although they had different personalities—Stella being realistic, practical, and independent and Vivian being needy, clingy, and almost living in a fantasy world—they formed a friendship that became solid and unshakeable.

Charlotte immersed herself in everything that was collegiate. She felt that she had been sheltered her whole life, so college represented freedom for her. At every athletic event, every college-sponsored dance, and every debate, protest, or social function, you could find Charlotte. She remembered Barbara's advice. It was no surprise that she was elected president of the freshmen class and was the editor of the yearbook staff and the head cheerleader by her sophomore year. Charlotte's grade point average never suffered one bit because she knew how to prioritize. Monday through Thursday, she was the proverbial bookworm; she practically lived in the library. But when the weekends came, she knew how to have fun. Cheerleading afforded Charlotte the opportunity to be invigorated by the energy and enthusiasm of a crowd. She effortlessly became a popular student on campus and was included in most of the social functions. After a football game, the students would meet at the student union and rehash the game. Although she was a cheerleader, Charlotte knew very little about the sport. Oh, she knew what a touchdown was, but if someone asked her what constituted illegal contact or what garnered a five-point or ten-point penalty, she was at a loss. But one girl in particular could hold her own with anyone doing a play-by-play analysis of why the team won or lost. Her command of the sport and her knowledge of statistics were astounding. She proved to be a little too loud for Charlotte's taste, but she still fascinated her.

When the discussion at the student union abated and the crowd thinned, the students would pair off and disperse, but Florence would usually be left standing alone. Charlotte felt a little sorry for her.

One evening, Charlotte decided to check out the debate team. When she got to the meeting, the only person she recognized was the loudmouthed girl who had demonstrated great debate skills after a football game. She quickly crossed the room to warmly welcome Charlotte.

"Hi! Glad you came. I'm Florence Spencer, vice president of the debate club."

"Thanks. I'm Charlotte, Charlotte Timmons, sophomore," replied Charlotte.

"And head cheerleader," added Florence. "You are good."

And from that brief meeting, a friendship was born.

Charlotte, Florence, and Stella were among the many students who could be seen at every protest, rally, or demonstration that involved social injustice. Vivian, on the other hand, was so self-centered, and like Victoria, Florence's first roommate, she spent her time outside the classroom, trying to find a husband.

Florence discovered that Charlotte actually lived in the same dorm as she did—the honors dorm. This meant that Charlotte was a serious student—much to the surprise of Florence. She thought the pretty cheerleader was there to get a husband as well and not an education. They learned more about each other when they were paired on the debate team. Each was impressed by the other's quick intellect. Florence never felt that Charlotte looked down her nose on her meager wardrobe, and Charlotte deeply appreciated the friendship generously given by Florence. They became friends, went to football games together, and often ate together in the cafeteria. They immersed themselves in college life, attending all the activities—particularity sorority and fraternity parties even though neither joined a campus sorority. During the second semester of their sophomore year, Charlotte and Florence decided to move from the honors dorm to the general sophomore dorm so they could be with a more sociable crowd. As Providence would have it, they became suite mates with Stella and Vivian.

Charlotte, Florence, Stella, and Vivian became inseparable. When you saw one, you saw the others. It was one for all and all for one. You would have thought that they shared the same mind until it was time for class. They were independent women with separate interests and beliefs, but they developed a deep and unshakable friendship that was born out of loyalty and respect.

Stella was the beauty queen of the bunch. They were all attractive women, but Stella was, as her friend Calvin often said, a "smoker." He classified women into three categories: brick houses, big-legged mamas, and smokers. A smoker was a combination of the first two. The great thing about Stella was that she knew she was pretty but never tried to outshine the others. Florence was the warrior of the group. She was loud, fearless, and honest, and whatever was on her mind came out of her mouth.

Vivian was the romantic—always operating in a semifantasy world and determined to have life as she thought it should be, regardless of the consequences. Charlotte was the group's conscience—constantly following the rules and always ready with sound advice for others but often neglecting that same advice for herself.

"Get up, Viv! Why are you still in bed? Don't you have a trig test this morning?" questioned Stella.

"I decided to sleep in today. Is that a crime?" snapped Vivian.

"Well, excuse the *h-e-double l* out of me for caring!" snapped Stella.

"Sorry, I am just getting over a little headache—that's all," apologized Vivian.

"And you look terrible. Are you running a fever? Your forehead is warm and sweaty. Girl, I am calling Charlotte, and we are taking you to the infirmary. You need a doctor."

"Please, please don't call Charlotte, Stella," begged Vivian. "I already saw a doctor, and he took care of it and gave me some antibiotics. I just need to rest. Just don't call Charlotte, please,"

"Antibiotics for a simple headache?" questioned Stella.

After giving Vivian a long, piercing look, Stella said, "All right, I won't call Charlotte. But if those antibiotics don't work on that 'headache' by tomorrow morning, I am personally taking you to the hospital."

Vivian didn't protest.

"By the way," continued Stella, "where *is* Albert? I am sure he is the one who gave you that headache. I haven't seen him for a couple of weeks."

"Oh, he's around. We decided to put a little space between us. See other people."

"And I am sure it was his idea to put that space between the two of you after he found out about your headache," sneered Stella.

Stella and Vivian were inseparable for the next few weeks, and they avoided Charlotte and Florence at all costs. Stella explained that she was tutoring Vivian in French, for which Charlotte and Florence had no interest. Both had passed their foreign-language requirements during their first semester.

After a few weeks, Vivian was back to her old self: confident, controlling, and vain and with an energetic and optimistic view of a future that she was determined to have. Stella realized for the first time that underneath Vivian's devil-may-care attitude dwelled a truly fragile girl with no idea of her worth. She was so desperate to climb the social ladder that she was willing to do anything, give up anything, and believe anything. From that day forward, Stella purposed to be Vivian's confidant, mentor, and protector.

CHAPTER 8

Hard Decisions

S HE JUST COULDN'T be pregnant—not Charlotte. She was only with Walter that one time. The death of her mother was too much to bear, and she just wanted to feel. And Walter was there. Walter was always there. From the time Charlotte arrived at the college, Walter was there. He helped her move her suitcases and stuff from the trunk of her mother's station wagon up the stairs to her second-floor dorm room. He was on the band and had to report to campus early, so when he saw them struggling, he volunteered to provide assistance. Charlotte and Walter became instant friends. Even Charlotte's mother fell in love with him. Rose secretly sized Walter up and mentally tried him on as a son-in-law. *Not bad,* she thought.

Since Charlotte was a cheerleader and Walter was a drummer in the band, they had many opportunities outside the classroom to develop a deep and lasting friendship. They served on the student council and were members of the debate team. Walter even sought Charlotte's approval for his girlfriends. If Charlotte didn't like one, she didn't stay around long, and vice versa for Charlotte's boyfriends.

Two years after her college graduation, Charlotte called her sister, Barbara, to let her know that their mother, Rose, was not feeling well and had been admitted to the cardiac ward of their local hospital. Along with emphysema, Rose had a history of heart disease that resulted from contracting rheumatic fever as a child. Barbara rushed home to be with her mother. The prognosis from the doctor was not encouraging. He said that Rose Timmons's heart was just wearing out. After about two days in intensive care, Rose Timmons's spirit left this world and followed the same path as her husband.

"I guess we are orphans now, Charlotte," announced Barbara.

As soon as she called Stella, Florence, and Vivian, they dropped everything and came to comfort her. Once the funeral was over, her friends returned to their lives, and Charlotte and Barbara stayed another week to settle their mother's estate. After Barbara left to join her family, Charlotte suddenly realized she was totally alone.

Although she was a daddy's girl, she realized that her mother's death was harder to bear than her father's because her mother had been there to help her get through it. Who would help her this time?

Walter called her that evening.

"I am just checking on you, Charlotte. You looked lost at your mother's funeral. I know Barbara left today, and you shouldn't be alone. My conference is ending, and I can be there in an hour and a half. Love you."

He hung up before she could protest.

When Walter arrived, he was carrying food and wine. Charlotte told him that she appreciated his gesture but was not in the mood for company.

"'Company'? You calling me 'company'?" asked Walter. "Don't insult me. Girl, you know I'm family. I know Mama Rose was sizing me up for her son-in-law." He smiled. "And seriously, I know how you don't eat when you are stressed."

Walter reminded Charlotte that he respected and loved Mama Rose and knew she would not want her baby girl to be alone that night. He was not taking no for an answer and would not leave his best friend alone. He would stay with her as long as she needed him.

And with that, Charlotte surrendered to the consolation and warmth that Walter liberally gave without reservations.

That was three weeks ago. Charlotte made a doctor's appointment to address the upset stomach that had been plaguing her for the last few days. She suspected it was food poisoning that was caused by the chicken-salad sandwich she bought from the new fast-food restaurant off the highway.

"Pregnant," she heard the doctor say.

"That can't be!" argued Charlotte. "I don't even have a boyfriend!"

"Well, young lady, if you only knew how many times I have heard that in this office," offered the doctor.

As she walked to her car, Charlotte was in a daze. Then, as if a light bulb went off, she remembered the night with Walter.

"*Oh no!*" she screamed so loud, people she had passed in the street turned around to see what the problem was.

When she got home, she picked up the phone to call Walter. *No,* she thought, and then she hung up the phone.

Then she tried calling Florence. *No.*

Then she tried calling Stella. She hung up before Stella answered.

Maybe Vivian? No, she will tell the others. And certainly not Barbara.

She remembered the advice Barbara had given her when she dropped a box of condoms into her purse out of sight of their mother before they left her at the college for the first time: "Remember, Sis, practicing safe sex is better than making hard decisions."

"Oh, Mama," Charlotte cried, "what am I going to do?"

The girls were busy with their lives, focusing on careers and relationships. Charlotte remembered that her grandmother would warn her to never get too busy to make memories while she was young because they are all she will have when she gets old. And she would have known; she lived until ninety-five. Charlotte passed that advice on to her friends, and as a result, they agreed to start going on vacations together to make memories. The rules were simple. One of the friends was responsible for planning the outing. They started in alphabetical order. Charlotte was first, Florence was second, Stella was third, and Vivian brought up the rear, and then they would start all over again. The person planning the vacation would select the destination, make the reservations, plan the itinerary, and manage the money. Each friend made a monthly deposit into the vacation savings account so that when it was time to go, money was no object. A critical component of the agreement was that everyone would have to accept whatever decision the one in charge made with no complaints. Since Charlotte's name came first, it was her turn.

She had selected Chicago during the month of November. They all knew that Charlotte loved the cold and thought winter fashions were the most glamorous. To Charlotte's advantage, it would be easier to camouflage her four-month pregnancy with loose sweaters and scarves. If no one noticed, she would say nothing. If she was questioned, she would confess. They had a pact to never lie to each other.

Since Walter was in Chicago, Charlotte decided to tell him about the pregnancy before she met with her friends. It had been four months since Walter had comforted Charlotte after the death of her mother. They had not had any contact since then, but Charlotte decided that she owed it to Walter to let him know. She called him and told him she would soon be traveling to Chicago and would love to get together with him over dinner. She had some news that she wanted to share with her good friend. Walter seemed excited and said he was anxious to see her as well. Charlotte arrived at the restaurant first and only had to wait fifteen minutes before Walter arrived. As usual, they were happy to see each other, and after a warm embrace, they placed their orders. Charlotte began by thanking Walter for getting her through the rough time after her mother's death.

He brushed it off, winked, and said with a smile, "What are friends for?"

The server brought their entrées, and as soon as they finished and before Charlotte could begin, Walter's face lit up, his smile covering his whole face, and he announced, "I can't hold my news any longer, Charlotte. Congratulate me! I am engaged! Can you believe it?"

"Engaged?" questioned Charlotte.

And with that, she knew she couldn't tell him. She had to move on.

CHAPTER 9

New People, Places, and Things

TWO YEARS LATER, the girls met in late fall, but this time, Florence chose New York City. Florence was on fall break, Charlotte had vacation, Vivian actually had a conference in town, and Stella—well, Stella was between jobs.

New York City was exciting in the fall—with just the right amount of chill in the air to justify wearing the fur capes that were so popular with the jet-set crowds. When everyone had arrived and unpacked, they made plans to hit the clubs and celebrate until the wee hours of the morning. Arriving fashionably late at Traps in Manhattan, they found a table near the bar and ordered their favorite drinks: white wine for Charlotte, sloe gin fizz for Vivian, whiskey sour for Florence, and of course, a cosmopolitan for Stella.

"Why don't you ever try something different, Charlotte? Always white wine," said Stella.

"But I like white wine. What's wrong with it?"

"There's nothing wrong with it. Just try something different. If you don't, you will never know what you are missing."

"All right, Stella, when we order the last round, I will try something different."

"I'm going to hold you to that, Charlotte."

Stella then turned to Vivian. "What's wrong with you? You haven't said anything for the last ten minutes. Get your head out of the clouds. You must have finally trapped a man."

Vivian just smiled and then said, "Girls, I think I am in love."

"What do you mean?" asked Florence. "You holding out on us, Viv?"

Vivian began telling them all about her new boyfriend—Herman A. Washington III. They met at the law office of Jones, McKinley, Newton, and Harrison. Vivian was using her lunch hour to deliver some statistical reports to the office manager when Herman inadvertently bumped into her, causing her to drop the contents of the folder she was carrying along with her apple and a ham-and-cheese sandwich. Herman apologized, and after seeing her scrambling after her apple, he felt obligated to invite her to lunch. Vivian declined and said she would take a rain check. Two days later, she called in her rain check, and the rest was history. They had dated twice a week for the last three months.

"I think he is the one," said Vivian. "His family has status and money, and his father is in politics. I think he is planning to run for elected office in the near future."

"When are we going to meet him?" they all asked in unison.

"Well," said Vivian, "he invited me to go with him to dinner with his family in two weeks. If they like me—well, who knows?"

"Maybe you will get that house with the picket fence, the two and a half kids, the dog, and the station wagon you've been telling us about for the last six years. I don't see why you are in such a hurry to get tied down," cautioned Stella.

The girls talked until the bar called for last rounds.

"All right, Charlotte, it's time for you to try something different." Stella turned to Charlotte.

"Maybe next time. It is getting late. I just want a cup of coffee."

"Then coffee is exactly what you shall have."

Stella went to the bar and ordered something for Charlotte.

"Here's your coffee, Charlotte. Drink up."

After taking a sip, Charlotte said, "Stella, this is quite good. What is this?"

"Just your 'special coffee,'" winked Stella.

Back at the hotel, the girls continued sharing intimate details of their lives as only good friends can, each keeping safe those few details that stay hidden in the deep recesses of the heart.

Stella had always been an early riser and quietly went to the kitchen the next morning to make coffee. When she turned on the light, she was almost startled when she saw Charlotte sitting at the kitchen table.

"Girl, you scared me! What are you doing, sitting here in the dark?" asked Stella.

When Charlotte turned around, Stella could see that she had been crying.

"What's wrong, Charlotte?"

"I can't sleep. I was just thinking about my mother and how much I miss her." Charlotte continued crying. "I really need to talk with her."

"Well, I know I am not your wonderful mother. I only met her twice, but to me, she was the epitome of motherhood. She talked with me, and I felt so much better. But if you need an ear, you know I am always here for you," offered Stella.

So Stella sat down and listened as Charlotte unburdened her heart and released some of the pain that had imprisoned her spirit; both understood that what was being said would stay between the two friends.

The weekend was over much too fast, and then each woman retreated back to her life.

The next time the four friends were all together was on the occasion of the wedding of Ms. Vivian Miller Anderson to Mr. Herman Anthony Washington III.

CHAPTER 10

The World of Work

Florence

FLORENCE GRADUATED IN May, and by August of that year, she started a career as a public-school teacher—one that lasted more than forty years. Her first teaching job was that of a first-grade teacher at Clear Creek Christian School, located just twenty-five miles north of Florence's hometown. Florence discovered that she really did love teaching in spite of the pushy parents, unruly kids, and insufficient budgets. She threw herself into her work with the same zeal she employed in college. In addition to teaching the twenty-five students of her class, she had bus duty, hall duty, and cafeteria duty. She was always the first to arrive at school. She needed to center herself before the first students arrived so she could greet them with a smile and an encouraging word. Her school day started at around 7:30 a.m. and didn't end until after 4:00 p.m. But she wouldn't have it any other way.

Florence found an apartment about ten miles from her family; she would have been happy to stay home for a few years and save some money for a down payment on a house, but Eleanor never offered.

After only six months of living on her own, Eleanor begged Florence to move back home. She could save money for the down payment on a house she wanted. Florence was so pleased that her mother missed her. They never really bonded before, and Florence was so starved for any crumb of affection from her mother that she jumped at the chance to move back home.

Once she was back, Florence went to see Pastor Robinson to thank him for all his support and let him know she was back home and would be available to serve in the church in any capacity. Pastor Robinson was more than pleased to see Florence and asked her what she had been doing since she graduated from college. At the end of their conversation, Pastor Robinson invited her to pick up where she left off with serving in the church.

"Thank you so much, Pastor," Florence responded. "You have always been so kind to me, just like Daddy was."

"Well, Florence," replied Pastor Robinson, "I know how much George loved you, and years ago, he asked me to promise that if you ever needed anything and he was not around, I would be there for you."

"Thank you, Pastor. You have certainly been there for me," said Florence.

Two days later, Florence had another encounter with Pastor Robinson. Her car had broken down on her way to work. Just as she stopped and popped the hood, Pastor Robinson drove up to her.

"Good morning, Florence. What seems to be the problem?"

"Good morning, Reverend. I don't know what is wrong with this car. This is the third time it has stopped this month."

Pastor Robinson looked under the hood, completed a diagnosis, and said, "Florence, this car is about shot. Why don't you get a new one? I know you haven't spent all your daddy's life-insurance money."

"Excuse me?" said Florence. "Insurance money? What money?"

"The $200,000 life-insurance policy that your father took out for you when you were ten. He often bragged that even though you were as smart as a whip and you would probably marry some rich college man, he wanted to make sure his baby girl would never have to beg anyone for anything if he wasn't around. Not that I was trying to be nosy, but I made sure for George's sake that Harry Smith deposited your insurance check at the bank as soon as it arrived."

This was the second time Florence heard something about an insurance policy her father had taken out for her benefit. Florence just stood there as Rev. Robinson continued discussing the $200,000. When he noticed that Florence had not said a word and had a confused look on her face, he realized that he had said too much.

"I am sorry. I may not have my facts straight. Please forget what I said," pleaded Rev. Robinson. "Let's just call Ray's Towing and get you to work."

Florence had her car towed to the nearest garage, and she sat in silence as Rev. Robinson gave her a lift to school. That day, Florence kept thinking about the $200,000 that she knew nothing about.

As soon as school was over, Florence picked up her car from the garage and drove directly to the bank; she was aware that she was speeding, but she had to get to the bank before it closed to speak to Mr. Smith, the bank manager. She had to find out about the insurance money.

Harry Smith confirmed what Rev. Robinson said earlier. George took out life insurance on himself for $200,000 with $50,000 going to Eleanor and $150,000 going to Florence. When he died, the money was deposited in the bank. Eleanor got the $50,000 immediately, and the remaining $150,000 was to be distributed at the rate of $50,000 annually on Florence's birthday, beginning when Florence turned eighteen. He said Eleanor came into the bank each year for the last two years on Florence's birthday with a note to withdraw $50,000, which she said was at Florence's request. The account had $50,000 left. Mr. Smith said Eleanor had called this very morning, inquiring about withdrawing the last $50,000 early because she said that Florence needed it this time before her birthday because she wanted to make a down payment on a house.

"You did request the money, didn't you, Florence?" asked Henry Smith.

"Just put a block on the account until you hear back from me, please, Mr. Smith," said Florence.

"Sure thing, Florence," said Mr. Smith, looking perplexed.

And with that, Florence left the bank without saying another word.

Eleanor, her own mother, had stolen $100,000 of the money her father left for her. *What did she do with it?* Florence thought.

Florence remembered receiving a certified letter from an insurance company that was for F. Anderson, but as soon as she signed for it, Eleanor practically tore it out of her hand and said it was intended for

E. Anderson. And there was the summer when Florence discovered new living-room furniture, televisions in each room, and a state-of-the-art grill in the backyard. She was really surprised to find a carport with a new car parked there, and her mother didn't even have a driver's license at the time. When she asked her mother how she could afford all the new things, Eleanor explained that she and the other children living at home were working and were pooling their monies to buy some of the finer things in life. Florence was happy for her family, although none of them offered up a penny to help her with her tuition.

Florence decided not to mention anything about the life-insurance money to her mother. She could tell that Eleanor had been to the bank and knew Mr. Smith had told her that Florence had put a block on the account. It was enough that her mother knew that she found out what happened to her money. At least her father had a funeral that was worthy of his memory.

Florence and her mother became even more distant. Her family continued to treat her like an outsider. She never took much pleasure in drinking for drinking's sake, and it was all her siblings seemed to want to do. Therefore, she dedicated her time to her students. Her only social outlet was her service to the church, and her only confidant seemed to be Pastor Robinson. He kept a good watch on Florence and would often ask her how things were going. One Saturday morning, Pastor Robinson asked Florence to accompany him to the food bank. On their way back, Pastor Robinson confided in Florence that his wife had left him over three months ago but he had not told the church. She took the two children with her and moved to Texas. Florence could see the sadness in his face but didn't know what to say. She felt so bad for him because he had always been there for her father and her. As Pastor Robinson continued talking and looking at her, Florence got the impression for a minute that Pastor Robinson was going to make a pass at her. She quickly but politely deflected the situation. Pastor Robinson was a very nice man, but Florence viewed him more as a father figure than as a potential suitor.

Two months after Florence moved back home, her mother and her siblings lost their jobs. Eleanor told Florence that since she was the only one working, she would need to take over the bills for a little while. She knew her mother was trying to retaliate for her finding out about the insurance money. "A little while" turned into a way of life.

Florence was quickly promoted to assistant principal. She was bringing in a good salary and wanted to buy a house but was only able to save a little bit of money because her mother and her siblings were always between jobs. For over two years, Florence was the only one getting up and going to work every day. She was getting tired of covering the mortgage, taxes, and groceries, and someone was always late with their car insurance. She drew the line when it came to buying beer and cigarettes.

One particular Sunday morning, as Florence was attending church services and enjoying the high energy singing that was coming from the choir, she began to miss her father because he always sang with the choir. She was not sad, just lonesome. Florence was getting tired of being the only one working and having to support everyone in the house. When Rev. Robinson began his sermon, he explained that he would speak on the sin of idleness. The biblical scripture he used was 2 Thessalonians 3:6–15 that explained that if you don't work, you don't eat. Florence knew this Word was for her and applied it to the situation with her family. Since her siblings chose not to work and spent their time on worthless activities (e.g., partying, drinking, drag racing, and the like), they would not be eating her food anymore.

The following Monday morning, seemingly out of the blue, Florence announced to her family that the First National Bank of Florence P. Anderson was closed and its headquarters was moving 350 miles away to Atlanta, Georgia. All loans were forgiven, but there would be no more withdrawals, loans, or other forms of credit. Her family didn't believe her, especially the part about her moving all the way to Georgia. Except for an occasional trip to visit one of her college roommates, Florence did nothing but go to work and church. Florence knew the time had come for her to move on and stop enabling grown folk. After putting her family in shock, Florence called Vivian and told her of her plan to relocate to Atlanta, Georgia.

"Atlanta?" shouted Vivian. "What possessed you to move to the South? What's wrong?"

Florence explained that she realized that her family was suffocating her and, if she ever wanted to get a husband, she had to cut all of them loose. One thing about Florence—when she made up her mind, she didn't waste time.

Florence packed her bags and her books and drove all night, arriving in Atlanta just before rush hour. She stopped for a bite and then checked into a hotel and fell on the bed, exhausted. Florence got up early the next morning, grabbed a cup of coffee, and set out to find a job, armed with a glowing letter of recommendation from her previous principal.

Florence pulled into the parking lot of the first elementary school she came to, asked to speak with its principal, and landed a job all before eleven o'clock. After a quick lunch, she then drove around for about an hour and a half, surveying her new city. Around the next corner, Florence saw a quaint little house with a "For Rent" sign in its yard. She located the owner; gave him her résumé, the deposit, and the first month's rent; got the keys; and moved in before 5:00 p.m. There were no furnishings and no utilities. The only light she had came from a flashlight that she retrieved from the glove compartment of her car, and she used her grandmother's quilt as a mattress and her faux fur coat as a pillow. Florence went to sleep with such peace and awoke to a new day and a new life.

As soon as her phone was installed, Florence called Charlotte, Vivian, and Stella. The next call she made was to Pastor Robinson, thanking him for all his support and concern over the years. She gave him her contact information in case there were any questions regarding any of the church activities she managed. Pastor Robinson was surprised and disappointed that she moved to Atlanta and made her promise to stay in touch so he could keep his promise to her father.

Charlotte

Charlotte told everyone that the reason she took the nursing internship in Arizona after her mother died was because she needed a change of scenery so she could grieve in her own way. After the ten-month internship was over, Charlotte returned to her mother's house.

"Arizona was just too hot for me. The heat seemed to have zapped my energy. I am happy to be back," she told her friends when she returned.

Once she was at home, Charlotte started aggressively looking for a nursing position. She discovered that she was still a little tired but needed to be around people so she wouldn't have to think about the events of "Arizona". Charlotte was eating the last of the leftovers she had put in the refrigerator the night before when a call came from the personnel office of Peace Hospital in Charlotte, North Carolina. It was only a few hours from the mountains, a few hours from the beach, and a few hours from her home. Besides, it was her namesake. As soon as she hung up the phone, she began shouting "Thank you, God!" and dancing her happy dance.

When Charlotte reported to work, she was outfitted with her white dress, white hose, and little white cap. She understood the line of demarcation between nurses and doctors. Protocol required nurses to stand and give up a chair when a physician entered the unit and at times fetch coffee if requested. She naturally got along well with the patients and the entire hospital staff, and it only took her a month to organize a birthday club. After only eighteen months of working a rotating schedule, Charlotte was promoted to the coveted day shift. It was on the first day of her day shift that she met Dr. Dawson Wright, the fresh-out-of-medical-school neurosurgeon. She immediately got up when he came behind the nurses' station, but he insisted that she stay seated, flashed his pearly whites, and winked at her. He seamlessly proceeded to focus his undivided attention on the patient's chart, mentally synthesizing the data so he could recommend an appropriate patient-treatment regimen. Charlotte was so impressed by Dr. Wright's demeanor that she brought him coffee even before he asked. "Thank you, Nurse Timmons. I really needed that."

Charlotte smiled and answered, "You're welcome, Dr. Wright. Can I get you anything else?"

"I'm good," replied Dr. Wright with another smile.

Dr. Wright was the youngest neurosurgeon to be hired at Peace Hospital. His work in the area of radiosurgery for the treatment of epilepsy was very promising. There was even an article on his research in the medical and trade magazines.

Charlotte liked Dr. Wright from the day she met him. It was his smile. It invited you into his personal space. She learned that he was born in Germany because his father had been in the military. His family returned to their hometown of Mobile, Alabama, after his father's discharge. His parents still lived there along with his two brothers and three sisters. He graduated third in his class and was one of the youngest neurosurgeons the hospital had ever hired. He enjoyed jazz and chess and was a smooth dancer. Charlotte learned all of these from listening to break-room gossip volunteered mostly by the night nurses Randal Jackson and Cybil Morgan. It was widely known that Cybil was doing everything she could to get Dr. Wright to notice her. And it worked because Cybil and Dr. Wright began dating.

Charlotte was not exactly sitting at home and twiddling her thumbs. She had a standing Friday-night date with George Kaufman, an up-and-coming police detective. The relationship was going quite well, but maybe that was because they spent very little time together due to their hectic work schedules. When they finally had a few days off at the same time, they realized they had nothing—absolutely nothing—in common. They didn't like the same food and hated each other's music, and their attitudes on having children ranged from zero to four. At least they agreed that the relationship was going nowhere and parted as friends.

Vivian

Graduating from college was a major accomplishment for Vivian, but the whole experience fell a little short because she did not find that husband she so desperately wanted to find, although she really tried. *Time to move on and look for a job. Maybe that's where my husband will be waiting for me.* This thought lifted her spirits.

Vivian majored in business administration to guarantee that she would get a job where her coworkers would predominately be successful men. She could not understand why Florence would want to be a public-school teacher whose colleagues were mostly underpaid women. *Charlotte might be on the right track and snag herself a doctor, and Stella— maybe she'll get a major movie star.* But she was in the market for a husband who was a financial mogul, a bank president, or a CEO—that would guarantee her financial stability and happiness. That's where she would do her job hunting.

Vivian examined all the want ads, and a job announcement for an executive secretary at the law firm of Jones, McKinley, Newton, and Harrison in Charleston, South Carolina, caught her eye. The job required supporting high-level executives. The term *high-level* equated to "high salary" to Vivian. Of course, typing, scheduling, writing correspondence, routing calls, greeting visitors, and answering questions and requests according to policy would be expected.

That was the one. With her best navy suit and heels on, her attaché case with her résumé under her arm, Vivian left to find her *knight in shining armor.*

Stella

Stella sold many of her personal designer clothes a month before graduation so she could buy her ticket to California. The talent scout promised that he had auditions lined up and waiting for her. Stella felt she had nothing to go back home for, so she set out to live her dream. *Look out, Hollywood! Stella is on the way!*

While Charlotte was deciding between two nursing job offers, Vivian was interviewing for an executive-secretary position at a prestigious law firm, and Florence had already signed a contract to teach first grade, Stella was just getting introduced to the world of Hollywood. She learned that her talent agent, Sam Carson, was also the agent for three other recent college graduates that he recruited along with her. Because Hollywood is an expensive place, Sam found his four recruits a low-rent apartment that they could share in Culver City, a suburb of Hollywood. He promised all the girls that he had auditions lined up for them, and they were anxious to become the next big stars. All four of them gave him $1,000 each for his services. Stella found out that running from one audition to another was hard work. It did not help that all her roommates auditioned for the same part. It took Stella two months to land a commercial for a dog-food product, but she was happy to take whatever job she could get. And it didn't pay well. By the end of the first six months, two of her roommates had given up and moved back home. Stella was determined to not let the industry beat her. Besides, she did not have a plan B. This was it. Stella learned firsthand two valuable lessons: Hollywood was not as glamorous as she imagined in college, and hard work does not always guarantee success. She had never worked as hard as she was working now. Stella also found out that the saying "It's not what you know but who you know" applied in Hollywood as well. After two more months, her last roommate moved out, and Stella knew she could not afford the rent by herself. So she took a job as a bartender at a local bar. She was pretty enough and friendly enough and made a great cocktail; she brought in enough tips to meet the rent. She would audition during the day and bartend at night. After Stella's last roommate left, Sam started coming around more often, and their business relationship turned into a romantic one. It wasn't that Stella was in love with Sam; it was just that she was so lonely. Sam began sending Stella on jobs that were questionable, but he specialized in being tenaciously persuasive, and his negotiation skills proved to be more than Stella could withstand.

"Sometimes you need more than talent to open Hollywood doors," Sam would often say.

She reluctantly followed Sam's advice. After all, he was the talent agent, and she had put her trust in him. She had no one else.

CHAPTER 11

A Fairy Tale Bride

I T TOOK THREE years before all four friends were together in one place since their last get-together in New York City. The occasion was the wedding of Ms. Vivian Joyce Anderson to Mr. Herman Anthony Washington III.

Charlotte was the last to receive the call from Vivian that she was getting married in three months. She had heard it initially from Florence, who seemed a little skeptical about the whole thing.

"Don't let her know that I already told you. She finally trapped Herman. They are officially engaged and getting married. I don't know how she managed that because he has been making excuses for the last three years. I sure hope she knows what she is doing. That family seems a little pretentious to me. But then again, so is Viv."

Charlotte promised to be surprised when Vivian called.

It was not until the next day that Vivian finally called Charlotte, and as if on cue, Charlotte screamed with delight at the news. Vivian excitedly recounted almost word for word to Charlotte every detail of Herman's perfect proposal.

"It happened just as I had always envisioned since I was thirteen," began Vivian. "I had gone to visit Herman in New York while he was at a business meeting. After we had dinner in Manhattan at this little French restaurant, Herman insisted that we go for a stroll in Central Park. After walking hand in hand and laughing for about fifteen minutes, we stopped, and Herman actually got down on one knee, pulled a black velvet box from his pocket, and popped the question right in front of everyone.

"He said, 'Vivian, love of my life, will you make all my dreams come true and be my wife?'

"I was swept off my feet and said 'Yes! Yes!' He said he didn't want to wait and wanted to get married as soon as possible. Then we kissed for what seemed like an eternity. People around us just clapped and clapped. It was so exciting. I finally found my knight in shining armor."

She had previously told the same exact story word for word to Florence and Stella, not deviating a single bit. It sounded like a rehearsed fairy tale, but it nevertheless left the girls very happy for Vivian. Of course, the girls would be bridesmaids with Stella as the maid of honor since she and Vivian had been college roommates since their freshman year. It was only in their junior year that Florence and Charlotte joined them.

The girls were almost as excited as Vivian as they helped her plan the most perfect wedding that Charleston, South Carolina, had ever witnessed. Vivian selected champagne and burgundy as her color scheme since she was having a winter wedding and felt confident that her choice of bridesmaid dresses would complement each girl's physical structure—from Stella's five-foot-nine curvy figure to Florence's five-foot-four hourglass figure to Charlotte's five-foot-six athletic figure. Florence's and Charlotte's dresses had high necklines, but Stella insisted that her dress allow as much cleavage as was decent.

After a number of phone calls that finalized details, Vivian's special day finally arrived. The girls came two days early in case their dresses needed alterations. Stella flew in from California; Charlotte, from North Carolina; and Florence, from Georgia. Winters in Charleston are usually mild, but when Stella stepped off the plane and breathed in the crisp December air, she knew she was not in California. Charlotte's flight arrived at the same time as Stella's, and as they shared a taxi ride to Vivian's house, they had a chance to catch up. Charlotte had recently ended a relationship of three years with a postal worker and had sworn off men altogether. Stella was still dating her agent but did not seem happy.

By the time they got to Vivian's house, Florence was already there, standing on the steps with Vivian, the two of them practically screaming as they recognized Charlotte and Stella. When they all got inside, they continued the screams of joy, hugs, and laughter as they toasted Vivian's big day with unending mimosas.

"Now where is my gorgeous dress?" said Stella. As she pushed up her breasts, she teased Vivian, "These girls have been exercising daily to upstage the bride."

Vivian looked awkward. "Well, there has been a little change—just a little change."

Just then, a woman who appeared to be in her late forties came in the room in a flowing lounge pantsuit, looking like a desperate homemaker trying to hold on to her youth.

"Girls, I would like you to meet Herman's mother, Mrs. Constance Carrington Washington II—or Mrs. Constance, as she likes to be called."

They all smiled said "Hello" in unison.

By the way Constance entered the room and acknowledged them, they knew she was some piece of work. She managed to grunt a muffled "Hello," looked them up and down as if with a magnifying glass, and in no uncertain terms, deflected their attempts at hugs, handshakes, or any other form of physical contact.

Almost on cue, Marianne, Vivian's mother, came into the room while carrying one of the bridesmaid dresses.

"And of course you all know my mother, Marianne."

"Mrs. Marianne!" said Florence, Stella, and Charlotte in unison with genuine delight as they hugged her. "It is so good to see you!"

"And it is good to see you girls as well," replied Marianne.

When Marianne laid the bridesmaid dresses across the bed, the girls noticed that they were different from the ones they had previously decided upon. Even the color was different.

Florence was the first to comment. "What happened, Viv? These are not the dresses we selected. And this color?"

"These are better for the Charleston crowd. You know the South requires modesty and good taste," answered Constance.

Vivian jumped in nervously, "And since Mrs. Constance is paying for the wedding—and it is going to be held at her house—it's only right that she is able to make a few changes—just a few."

"'Good taste'?" asked Florence. "What was wrong with the ones Vivian picked out earlier?"

"Dear, they were not adequate for the type of political circles Herman and Vivian will be running in with my husband slated to win his upcoming election. They were good enough, I imagine, for commoners, but high society? I think not," sneered Constance.

"'Commoners'? What the—"

Before Florence could complete her sentence, Stella and Charlotte quickly grabbed her by the arm and swiftly and forcibly led her to the other side of the room. Stella then said, "Now, Florence, the colors are nice, and the sizes are the same."

"Well, young ladies, try on the dresses and see if they need any alterations. If so, let my maid know."

She turned to Vivian and Marianne and in a commanding tone said "Come,."

The mothers and bride-to-be departed but not before Vivian looked back at the girls with an expression of desperation on her face.

You could almost see the steam coming from Florence. She didn't drink hard liquor because of her religion, but boy could she cuss—really cuss.

"What the —— just happened? Whose wedding is this anyway?"

"This is the *headness come off I ever saw*!" said Charlotte, slipping in one of her grandmother's old sayings.

"We all just need to calm down. After all, this is Viv's wedding, and she is the one who must deal with her soon-to-be mother-in-law and her new husband. If she can live with them, then we can live without them," reassured Stella.

After tempers cooled, they started trying on the dresses. Since all three dresses were the same style, Stella would not be able to show any cleavage. Charlotte and Florence were able to fit in their dresses fine, but Stella's needed altering because she had lost quite a bit of weight, which concerned Charlotte.

"Have you been eating?" quizzed Charlotte.

Stella flippantly replied, "You guessed it—I haven't been eating." "Seriously," she continued, "I have been on this new diet because you know, ladies, you can't be too rich or too thin."

Charlotte was still concerned because during their sophomore year in college, Stella had developed a voluptuous figure that delighted all the boys and was the envy of all the girls, but this thin figure of Stella's made her look almost emaciated. Even her "girls" looked like someone had let the air out of them because they looked like they went from a double D to an A.

"Just make sure you are taking vitamins with that diet. You don't want to become anemic."

"Yes, Nurse Charlotte," replied Stella sarcastically.

"All right, Florence," asked Stella, changing the subject, "what gives with that new fur coat? What are they paying teachers these days?"

"Two years of eating beans and hot dogs to save for the down payment" was Florence's reply. "You can't take it with you. I might as well get all I can before the husband and babies come."

"If they do come," said Stella with a smile.

"Can somebody tell me why Vivian is getting married here in Charleston? Why didn't she have her wedding in Philadelphia? That's where her mother and all her friends live." Charlotte added, "And especially since her Aunt Ruby can't fly because of her recent bypass surgery."

Florence was disgusted. "I think that Mother-in-Law is the one calling the shots. She is so controlling. Just because her husband is in politics, she thinks everything has to revolve around him. 'High society'! That is what I hate about these nouveau riche people—they are always trying to be something that they are not."

"Putting on airs," said Charlotte.

"Well, that Constance does take the cake."

"And have you ever seen such a sad-looking groom? I saw Herman briefly when we checked in, and he practically ignored me. I initially thought it was wedding jitters, but now I am not so sure. He looked like he was going to a funeral and not his wedding. I think I will have a little talk with him."

"This is none of your business, Florence. If Vivian wants to marry into this family, it's her decision. Leave it alone."

"Like hell I will, Charlotte. And you know I don't cuss. Vivian is our friend, and something just isn't right."

"Who doesn't cuss? I agree with you—something isn't right, but leave it alone."

"You know that when she makes up her mind, Charlotte, it's no use talking to her," whispered Stella.

That evening, the girls arrived at the wedding rehearsal at 6:30 p.m.—just as Constance and Herman Sr. arrived. The atmosphere was as icy as the temperature of the room. Somehow they got through it. Constance announced that she and Herman Sr. would stand in at the wedding rehearsal because Vivian and Herman Jr. were busy with getting ready for their big day. It seemed a little strange to the girls, but they were learning that Constance was the one running the show.

The wedding rehearsal went off like clockwork, and the bridal party retired to the sunroom for the rehearsal dinner.

Constance did know how to throw a great rehearsal-dinner party. With Vivian and Herman Jr. away, you would have thought it was Constance and Herman Sr.'s wedding. The food and wine flowed endlessly, and the photographer never ran out of film. Except for the usual toasts made to the absent bride-to-be and groom-to-be, you would have thought it was Herman Sr.'s political coming-out party. And Constance! She flittered and flirted with every man and complimented every woman's "exquisite" style while singing her husband's praises at the same time. It was like a campaign rally. The only thing missing was Herman Sr. kissing babies. At the conclusion of the rehearsal dinner, Constance announced that everyone should be on post for the wedding the next day. She expected nothing less than perfection.

The wedding started late because Vivian and Herman Jr. were nowhere to be found. After waiting for fifteen minutes, Constance whispered something into her husband's ear, and he went down the aisle to the front and apologized for the delay. Constance slipped out a side door. Trying to stall, Herman attempted to entertain the audience with jokes that were so dry they were almost funny. After another fifteen minutes of Herman Sr.'s excruciatingly painful jokes, he got the cue to go to the back of the church. As soon as he made it to the back, the wedding began, and it *was* perfect.

Vivian looked elegant, and her wedding gown fit her like a glove. She wore a plastic smile and suppressed any hint that this was not the perfect wedding between two perfect people who were deeply in love. The music, flowers, food, and everything else were available in abundance. Champagne flowed endlessly, and dancing went on for hours. The guest list read like a who's who of Charleston high society and beyond except almost everyone seemed to be over fifty and there were very few young people invited. Except for the girls, there were no other friends of Vivian in attendance.

Florence caught the bouquet although she wasn't exactly in the line. She never went out for such traditions. After the wedding, Vivian said goodbye to and hugged each one of her friends uncharacteristically long and desperately tight. She whispered to Florence to say a prayer for her, and then she went off on her perfect honeymoon with her perfect husband, just like Cinderella, both still wearing plastic smiles.

"Charlotte, you and Stella go ahead to the hotel. I'll be there in a minute. Got to run a little errand," Florence said.

"Don't put your nose where it doesn't belong, Florence."

"You all know me, Stella," replied Florence.

"Yeah, we do. That's why I said it."

When Charlotte and Stella arrived back at the hotel room, Charlotte ordered a midnight snack, although it was only 9:00 p.m. Since they had been on their feet all day and had early-morning flights back home, they decided to stay in. Charlotte and Stella started gossiping about Vivian's wedding as only true friends could. They still could not believe that Marianne had let Constance commandeer the wedding. It was true that life's ups and downs had molded Marianne into a woman with a humble and submissive temperament, but for her to passively allow the spotlight to turn from her only daughter's wedding to Constance's politicking was unbelievable. While Charlotte and Stella were pondering the situation, Florence came into the room in a whirlwind, threw her purse and wrap onto the bed, and said, "Well, I know the what, why, and who. And I am going to kill Viv when I get the chance. You know what that heffa has been up to?"

Charlotte and Stella both asked, "What?"

"Well, I just left Mrs. Marianne, and she started talking to me like I already knew that Vivian had been pregnant. Did the two of you know?"

"What do you mean 'had been pregnant'?" asked Charlotte.

"Mrs. Marianne said Viv told her a month ago that she had been pregnant and miscarried. But she wanted to wait and not tell Herman that she lost the baby until two days before the wedding. She was afraid he would call it off. Vivian has been chasing Herman these three years, but he was already engaged to his longtime girlfriend named Patricia. Because Vivian was pregnant, his mother made Herman marry Vivian to put down any scandal. She wanted nothing to jeopardize her husband's bid for mayor. Well, Vivian started getting cold feet and felt she should tell Herman about the miscarriage, so she told Herman just before we arrived. He accused her of trying to trap him in a loveless marriage, and he did not believe she had ever been pregnant. He demanded that Vivian produce medical information attesting to the pregnancy and miscarriage, and if she couldn't, there would be no wedding."

"Did Viv show him the medical records?" asked Charlotte.

"Are you kidding? What do you think? When she couldn't produce any documentation, Herman went to his mother to tell her the wedding was off. Constance told Herman it was too late to call it off because she had spent too much on the wedding and had invited all the prominent people from Charleston who could be instrumental in helping get her husband get elected. She told Herman to go along with the wedding and just divorce Vivian after the election is over. She was not going to put up with a scandal this close to the election. She told Herman to get separate rooms for their honeymoon and to not, under any circumstances, consummate the marriage. Constance knew the law.

"Constance had her lawyer meet with Vivian and Marianne and tell them he was aware of their scam and if they did not go along with Constance's plan, they would be sued for fraud and Constance would seek punitive damages for emotional stress. Constance decided to use the occasion of a formal wedding to introduce her husband as a viable candidate for mayor with no hint of scandal.

"Didn't you all notice at the reception how Constance paraded her husband around like a prized bull that she was trying to sell to the highest bidder? This wedding gave Constance an opportunity to display a level of sophistication she so desperately wanted to project," said Florence.

"Do you think Vivian was ever pregnant, Florence?"

"Stella, you know Vivian just as well as I do. I think she would do anything to marry into a family as prominent as the Washingtons— even fake a pregnancy. Her whole life has been one fairy tale after another."

"No wonder Herman never smiled or held Vivian's hand. Poor Vivian. A trapped man will eventually find a key and escape," sighed Charlotte.

Charlotte, Stella, and Florence got little sleep that night, worrying about Vivian. During breakfast the next morning, they managed to hold their peace and extend polite goodbyes to Constance and Marianne and head back to their respective lives. Florence did not forget to pray for Vivian and Herman because she knew they would need it.

CHAPTER 12

Return to Reality

B ACK FROM VIVIAN'S wedding, Charlotte reviewed all that had happened and started thinking seriously if she was willing to get married at any cost. As soon as she returned to work, her friend Betty told her that Dr. Wright and Cybil broke up and he had been asking everyone when Charlotte was getting back.

"Girl, I think he is really interested in you," Betty continued.

As if on cue, Dr. Wright turned the corner, smiling as he could not contain his happiness at seeing Charlotte.

"Welcome back, Nurse Timmons. Ready to go to the port city of Mobile? I heard you wanted to attend a Mardi Gras Carnival after your friend's wedding."

Charlotte had heard that Cybil and Dr. Wright were no longer dating, and she was cautiously pleased. "I do want to go to the Mardi Gras Carnival, but isn't it held in New Orleans, Louisiana?." Charlotte asked.

"Nurse Timmons, you may not be aware of it, but Mobile, Alabama, is the birthplace of Mardi Gras in America. If you want to participate in a celebration that is alcohol-fueled and lets you overindulge in debauchery of all kinds, then by all means go to New Orleans, but if you can appreciate a more wholesome atmosphere but still want the excitement of parades and balls, then try Mobile. I would be delighted to show you around."

And that encounter was the beginning of what turned out to be a wonderful life for Charlotte Timmons.

～

Thoughts of Vivian's wedding were still swirling around in Stella's brain when she returned home, She knew she had to find another part-time job because she *had* lost quite a bit of weight—not because she was on a new diet, as she said, but because she was practically starving. The salary from her waitress job was barely enough to make the rent for the run-down apartment she was living in. Sam promised her a quick rise to fame, but ever since they began dating, he seemed more interested in her as a girlfriend than as a client. She admitted to herself that she was only dating him to get ahead in the business but realized that his expertise as a talent agent was just as deficient as his expertise as a boyfriend. And he was cheap. There were no offers to help with the rent or to buy her anything. He was not like the men she saw constantly in the movies. Maybe she was not being realistic. Or maybe Vivian's fairy-tale mentality was rubbing off on her. He did find her a few auditions and actually landed her a part in two commercials, but the pay was little compensation for having to pretend that Sam was meeting her needs professionally and physically. And to "put icing on the cake," as Grandma Beulah would say, she found out that Sam was not supposed to charge her and her other roommates $1,000 each. He was only entitled to get paid a commission from the jobs he got for them. This knowledge made Stella angry, and she wasted no time in demanding her money back, and she got it. She also took her apartment key back and told him it was time for him to move on.

That was what was on her mind as she left a dead-end audition, and she was now on the way to the next one, which she booked herself at the last minute. As soon as she arrived, Stella was handed a script and asked to read for the part of Georgia, the maid. Stella didn't care what the part was. She just wanted to "be in pictures." Stella really nailed the audition, according to her, but for some reason, the part went to another woman who was much older than her. Usually, after a rejection, she would take a deep breath and convince herself that the next audition would be her big break. But after going through this routine for four years, Stella was tired. Maybe she was not meant to see her name up in lights. She decided to just go on working at Dizzy's and be content. As soon as she opened the door to the bar, Dizzy met her with a pink slip.

"You're late again, and you're fired," said Dizzy. "Didn't I tell you that if you were late again, you would be fired? I got to let you go, Stella."

After she collected herself, Stella smiled and gave the greatest impromptu performance of her young life. "I just came by, Dizzy, as a courtesy. I wanted to tell you I am sorry but I have to quit. I got a starring role in a new movie and won't have time to work here."

Stella forced herself to smile as she thanked Dizzy for the opportunity he gave her. Dizzy seemed a little disappointed that Stella did not beg for her job as she usually did when he threatened to fire her. But he believed that she had finally landed that big part and wished her good luck and told her that if she needed a reference, she could count on him.

As Stella turned to leave, with a sinking heart and an empty stomach, she realized she had no idea what she was going to do or what she was going to eat. When she arrived home, she sat down on the floor beside her bed and cried.

"Lord, I can use some of that favor if it is not all gone." She said "What am I going to do?" over and over until she fell asleep.

The phone rang, waking Stella out of a sound sleep. The clock read "5:35 a.m."

"Who is calling me this early?" she grumbled as she reached for the phone.

"Hello."

"Hey, Stella! Sorry, girl. I forgot it is still early in California, but I just had to call you. Guess where Florence is!"

Before Stella could answer, Vivian shouted, "South of the Mason-Dixon Line! In Georgia! She up and moved to Atlanta! Can you believe it?"

"Hold up, Vivian. In Atlanta? Am I still asleep? What is Florence doing down there?" asked Stella.

For the next thirty-five minutes, Vivian gave Stella the lowdown on Florence's return to the South. Vivian was excited that at least one of them had moved closer to her. After hanging up, Stella tried to go back to sleep, but her mind would not settle down.

Stella was happy for Florence but felt more alone than ever. California proved to be a popular destination for young professionals because it offered numerous microclimates with mild winters and dry summers. That was one of the reasons Stella landed here after graduation. Now, six years later, she lay in bed, contemplating her fate. She had no family, no man, no money, and no job, and believe it or not, for the first time in years, snow was falling. It was not a blizzard, but it was enough for Stella to know that even the weather had betrayed her.

She got up, took a shower, and fixed herself a cinnamon coffee before getting the last piece of her homemade banana bread from the refrigerator. There was always some magazine, newspaper, or book perched on the corner of her dining table that she read as she ate. As a consummate English major, this practice kept her mind sharp and her vocabulary rich. The closest book within reach was an anthology of quotations, and she opened it. After about fifteen minutes of reading, her eyes grew wide as her mind and spirit absorbed the emotional charge that came from a quote attributed to Francis Bacon: "Aut viam inveniam aut faciam," which generally means, "I'll either find a way or make one." *Hallelujah!* Florence would have called this Divine intervention. Maybe it was because Stella knew exactly what she had to do: Find a way out of this mess or make one herself. After all, she was Estella Louisa Miller—a young, attractive, and very intelligent college graduate.

Gulping down the last of her cold coffee, Stella took inventory. She had exactly $272.85 in her checking account and rent paid up for thirty days. It was now or never. She had to find a real job.

It was time for her to break out her emergency outfit, which she received as payment from a previous perfume commercial. The outfit consisted of a black Armani interview suit, a white vintage blouse, and black Cole Haan pumps. She dressed, threw her shoulders back, and went out the door. She was not going to look for a job; she was going to get one.

The sign read "Help Wanted." It hung over the door of an antiquarian bookstore named Printed and Painted Word, which was nestled indiscriminately between a doughnut shop and a guitar-repair shop. The bookstore was looking for a stockroom clerk/custodian who could keep the books dusted and shelved and would report to the store manager. Stella was tired, hungry, and desperate. She just wanted a job. As she entered the bookstore, the rich smell of old and new books was so thick that it conjured up a long-forgotten memory from her childhood when a group of girls from her class were bullying her for wearing her sisters' hand-me-downs. She sought refuge in the school library and saw a book on tie-dyeing. That particular incident was the impetus that stimulated her creativity in clothing design.

From the back room appeared the proprietor, a middle-aged gentleman with a slight limp. He had a head full of black and silver hair that set atop his olive colored face with noticeable wrinkles that testified of happy and sad times. His clear grey eyes had a delightful twinkle that told Stella that he was harmless.

Remembering the advice of her acting coach, she slowly and delicately extended her hand as she inquired about the job, using the thickest southern drawl she learned from Vivian. She flashed him a smile that promised more than she was willing to deliver as she handed him a copy of her résumé. He introduced himself as Salvatore Zito, or Sal for short, and proceeded to look her up and down but not in a sexual way. His eyes were fixated on her face and the white streak in her hair. Stella assured him she was not into disco or rock music and explained that the white hair was in fact a birthmark.

"Actually, classical music is my genre of choice," Stella explained.

"Sorry for staring," explained Sal. "It's just that you look remarkably like someone I have seen before. Her name was Annalisa. You have a striking resemblance to her."

"Sorry, I have never heard of her," replied Stella.

Sal proceeded to give Stella an application form, asked her to complete it, and told her to ring the bell when she was finished. He then returned to the back of the store.

Stella thought his behavior was odd but surmised that he was rather harmless, and she completed the job application. She rang the bell when she was finished as he had requested. And like magic, the proprietor reappeared. He perused the application while nodding his head. When he finished, he invited Stella to look around as he excused himself again and headed to the back office. This time, Stella could hear him on the phone, talking in a subdued tone. She guessed he was talking to Dizzy. She hoped Dizzy didn't say anything about her coming to work late. Stella was getting nervous because she really needed this job.

After about fifteen minutes, the "Help Wanted" sign was in the trash, and Stella was leaving with the keys to the front door. She was to begin working the next day.

CHAPTER 13

The Myth of Happily Ever After

T O THE OUTSIDE world, Vivian's life was perfect. She had the handsome husband, the furs and automobiles, the large house, and a beautiful child. She had quit working as soon as her daughter Jennifer was born. She really was not cut out for the corporate life anyway. She always envisioned herself as the perfect wife of a dotting husband, a stay-at-home mom with perfect children who lived the perfect life behind a white picket fence. But things did not turn out exactly how Vivian had planned. Her life was nothing like the fairy tale she invented for the outside world. For one thing, Herman was cold and distant. After he found out about the scheme that she had concocted to get him to marry her, he wanted nothing to do with her. But on their wedding night, after Herman was sufficiently drunk, and dismissing the advice of Constance, he took Vivian to bed in a spirit of spite and entitlement. He gave no warmth and felt he should get something for his trouble. Vivian had agreed to give Herman a divorce after a respectable six months of marriage, but two months into the marriage, she got pregnant. Vivian called Herman's mother and told her she was pregnant; this time, she sent her the report from her obstetrician. The divorce would have to be postponed until after the baby was born. Constance was secretly thrilled that she would be having a grandbaby. Her political mind went into overdrive as she envisioned her husband as a doting grandfather, an image that was sure to boost his political career. When Jennifer was born, Constance virtually took her from Vivian. She made all the decisions about her care, hired a baby nurse with no input from Vivian, selected the clothes she would wear and the toys she would play with, and even decorated a room at her house for her "Little Jennie," as she affectionately called her.

When the girls came to spend a weekend with Vivian so they could spoil their new niece, who was now six months old, LaLa, as she insisted Jennie call her as she believed she was too young to be called Grandma (that was relegated to Marianne), had taken her with her baby nurse on her first outing to Hilton Head, South Carolina, without getting permission from Vivian.

"What the hell?" yelled Florence. "Viv, for someone who has such strong math skills, your life skills sure are in the pits. Don't you see what that woman is doing? She is stealing your child. If you were willing to hang between life and death to bring that baby into this world, why would you let some other woman reap the benefits? And where is that no-good, spineless worm of a husband?"

"Enough, Florence—enough. When you get married and have a child, then you may have an opinion," said Stella. She turned to Vivian. "Good to see you, Viv. You know Florence—always putting her nose in other people's business."

"Oh, Florence knows I don't pay her any attention. Come, girls. Cocktails are ready," answered Vivian. "And for you, Florence, just straight ginger beer," Vivian said with a sneer.

And with that, the four friends shared a wonderful weekend of good food, great conversation, and honest and supportive fellowship.

But Florence was right. Constance stole Vivian's child. Not literally, but Constance gave Jennifer everything she could ask for before she asked for it. And if Vivian or Marianne objected, Jennifer would throw such a temper tantrum that everyone gave in. And Herman Jr. was no help because he was never home. By the time Jennifer was in elementary school, she had become self-centered, exhibited little respect toward Vivian, mimicked the behavior of Herman Jr. and Constance, and had acquired a spirit of entitlement.

CHAPTER 14

A Piece of the Puzzle

"I CAN'T BELIEVE we are actually in Venice, Italy!" yelled Florence. "'The city of bridges, canals, and great food'! That's what the brochure says, and it is right. This is wonderful. I am so glad you suggested that we come here for our biannual vacation, Stella. And, Vivian, we told you not to bring all that luggage. Who are you trying to impress? Certainly not us."

Getting to their apartment took a little effort. After the train let them out at St. Mark's Square, they had to cross the Ponte di Rialto, and everyone was beginning to feel a little sorry for Vivian, who was trying to maneuver the first forty-two steps up the ramp of the bridge with all her luggage in tow. It became obvious that Vivian would need help with going down the ramp, so her friends stepped in after giving her the threat that if she brought more than a carry-on on the next trip, they would leave her at the airport. Once they crossed the bridge, they had to take a water taxi and then go through a maze of gates and go up some stairs before they got to the apartment. Once they arrived and turned the key, they all breathed a sigh of relief and were extremely pleased with the accommodations. The great view of the canal from the rooftop terrace made up for all the inconveniences.

"You did good, Stella. How did you know this would be such a great apartment? You know we have gotten stuck with horrible hotel rooms over the years. Remember the one in Belize?" asked Charlotte.

"Let's forget that place," said Florence, "since you know I was the one who made the reservation."

"Well, ladies, I have an additional surprise for you. This apartment is free of charge," announced Stella.

"You've got to be lying, Stella!" exclaimed Florence. "How?"

"My boss, Sal, was offered this apartment—free of charge—for two weeks if he would come over and give a seminar at some obscure museum here. He said he could not go but if I would conduct the seminar, I could use the apartment for free. He knew I always wanted to travel to Italy. I never told him it was because I was born here to a single mother while she was a student at one of the universities. I also never told him how she died or that I was adopted by my aunt. I don't know why not. Sal has been like a father to me," confessed Stella.

"You mean we get two weeks in Italy for free?" asked Charlotte.

"That's right—two whole weeks," replied Stella. "The seminar is only for one day, so the remainder of the time, we can explore as much of the islands and the nightlife as is available."

After a good night's sleep, the girls started out to enjoy the area as tourists do. Their days were filled with gondola rides along the Grand Canal, café-hopping for coffee and wine, shopping at the markets around Rialto Bridge, and basking in the richness of the famous art museums.

The evenings were spent attending opera performances, touring Venetian cicchetti bars, listening to café live music, and going over to the mainland in Mestre to enjoy the lively nightlife.

The first week seemed to fly by, but the time had come for Stella to make her presentation at the small museum near the Università Iuav di Venezia. She had learned quite a bit about art expression from working so closely with Sal these last five years and was almost an expert in curation. Charlotte, Florence, and Vivian accompanied Stella and agreed to be her cheering squad. None of them had seen Stella in action in her element.

Stella was very impressive, and she took command of the seminar. As soon as she finished, a kind gentleman who looked remarkably like Sal came up to Stella and complimented her on her knowledge of the subject. He introduced himself as Mario Zito, a first cousin of Sal. Mario said Sal volunteered to do the seminar each year so he could get an all-expenses-paid vacation. After a good laugh, Mario invited Stella to dinner at his home for the following afternoon. She told him thanks but she was here on vacation with friends. Mario asked her to bring her friends along. "Don't eat before you come," he cautioned, "because the food will be magnificent and plenteous."

"How can I say no?" said Stella, and she accepted his invitation.

The girls were just as excited as Stella to dine at an authentic Italian table. As soon as they arrived at Mario's address, they were greeted by so many wonderful smells that they could hardly wait to be invited inside. When they knocked on the door, it was opened, to Stella's surprise, by not only Mario but also Sal, Stella's boss. After Stella recovered from the shock of seeing Sal, she introduced Charlotte, Vivian, and Florence to Sal, who in turn introduced them to the rest of the guests: his sisters, brothers, cousins, nieces, and nephews—all fifteen of them. Everyone greeted Stella and her friends warmly.

He then asked if he could steal Stella for a few minutes so they could discuss the seminar. Charlotte, Florence, and Vivian were invited to the rooftop to experience a wine tasting that used bottles from the family's private collection.

Sal led Stella into his study so they could look at his private art collection as he called it—pictures of his family. Some were in elaborate frames, some were in photo albums, and some were in boxes. Sal named each individual in each photo. This sharing of Sal's family took almost two hours, but Stella was not bored at all.

Stella had picked up a picture of a handsome young man. "Who is this?" she asked.

"That's my brother Luigi when he was about twenty-five years old," said Sal. "He is a bit older now, around sixty years old. He is the dean of the art department at a university in Rome and painted many of the works that hang on these walls. He still comes home every weekend and will be joining us later this evening. I told him all about you, and he is anxious to meet you."

"He teaches art in Rome?" asked Stella. "My mother attended college someplace in Europe many years ago. I think it was Italy."

"You never talked about your family, Stella, and I guess I never inquired. Where is your mother?"

"She died when I was only six months old. She was returning to America after studying abroad for two years. After getting off the plane in New York, she boarded a train to Philadelphia, and it hit an ice patch, and the train went off a cliff. She died along with other passengers, but by some miracle, I made it out without a scratch. So my aunt told me," recounted Stella. "That's really all I know."

"And you never investigated anything else about your mother?" said Sal.

"No, not really. My aunt only told me about my mother when I turned sixteen. Before that, I thought my aunt was my mother. Once I found out my life had been a lie, I just pushed all of it out of my mind. My real mother was dead anyway, and that chapter was over before it began. And I guess all I have of her is this birthmark that really freaked you out when you saw it. You thought I was some sort of hippie with streaked hair." Stella laughed.

"What about your father? Did your aunt tell you anything about him?"

"Nothing. She said she had no information whatsoever. She didn't even know my mother was pregnant. I found out that both my aunt and my mother were adopted and they were not even blood relatives. So you see, I am truly an orphan," said Stella sadly.

"Girl, you have family. The four of us are family," said Vivian as Stella's three friends walked into the room after hearing the last part of Stella's conversation with Sal.

"You know that is right," echoed Florence and Charlotte.

"I know, and thanks," said Stella.

"All right, ladies, dinner is served. Let's go before you four flood out my house," said Sal as he wiped his eyes.

When everyone was seated, all kinds of great-smelling foods were served. The girls' taste buds were really blown away. They could not remember when they had tasted such delicious and authentic Italian food. The menu consisted of spaghetti with tomato-and-lamb ragù, wild-boar sausage, cabbage, roasted potatoes with eggplant, and chunky prosciutto.

Florence couldn't resist asking, "Do you all eat like this every day?"

Sal smiled and said, "Usually."

Such a meal was not complete without a great, locally pressed Italian wine. The dinner ended with an indescribable chocolate sponge cake and coffee laced with a centerba liqueur, which Sal insisted they take in the garden.

As soon as they arrived in the garden, a handsome middle-aged man who definitely had to be Sal's brother started approaching them. As soon as he was in eyeshot, he dropped his glass, unaware that he was spilling his wine. He continued approaching the guests and was speechless for a noticeable moment.

Sal made the introductions, first introducing Charlotte and then Vivian and Florence and finally Stella. He then introduced his brother Luigi. As they all sat down, Luigi could not take his eyes off Stella. They made polite conversation, explaining how they had enjoyed their stay in Italy, what they loved about the country, and the hospitality of Sal and his family. Florence thanked their hosts on behalf of the others and explained that they would be leaving for America tomorrow night and hope to return. Sal asked Stella if she could stay a little longer to brief him on the seminar, and he promised Stella's friends that he would drive her back later.

When Charlotte, Florence, and Vivian returned to the hotel, they discussed the great evening, the scrumptious food, and the fact that Sal's brother could not keep his eyes off Stella—and at his age, although he was good-looking. They all laughed and got ready for bed.

Everyone met in the kitchen for coffee the following morning and noticed that Stella still had not come home. They discovered in a panic that none of them had Sal's number. Just as Florence picked up the phone to call the Italian police, Stella came through the door.

"Where the hell have you been, Stella? I don't care if Sal is your boss. We have been worried about you. And everyone saw how his brother Luigi—who, by the way, kept that hat on—never took his eyes off you the whole evening. What have you been doing all this time? You okay?" questioned Florence.

Stella's face broke into a big smile, and she told them that Luigi took his hat off and revealed the same white-streak birthmark that she has. She said Luigi was her father!

The plane ride back home was one filled with wonder and excitement. Stella was able to fill in some of the gaps in her life's story with her father's help.

Her mother, Grace, and her father, Luigi, met on the first day Grace arrived in Rome. They both had been accepted into a yearlong program for up-and-coming young artists from around the world. It was a grant to determine if art was an international language. Grace did not understand Italian, and Luigi knew no English, so they made a good pair. One of the things each student had to do was choose a name in the language of their partner, so Grace became Annalisa, and Luigi became Lewis. By the end of the year, each team was to complete an art project and have it evaluated. The team that won would get an extension for another year with a paid salary to teach the program for the upcoming group of artists. Annalisa and Lewis won and received the appointment. During this time, Luigi and Grace had fallen in love, had gotten married, and had a child. But to fulfill the requirements of the grant that allowed Grace to go to Rome, she had to return to America to give a face-to-face report to the awards committee about the end results of the experience. She also wanted to take the opportunity to see her sister and show off her new baby before she returned to resume her life with Luigi and their child.

Luigi never heard anything else from Annalisa. He assumed that she had a change of mind and decided not to return. He tried to find her for years but was looking for an Annalisa Miller and not a Grace Miller. After a while, he gave up and stopped looking. One day, he got a call from his brother, Sal, who said he saw a girl who looked just like Annalisa and applied for a job in his bookstore. He asked Stella if she knew anyone named Annalisa, and she did not, so he orchestrated the trip to Venice so Stella would come and Luigi could be sure she was his daughter. The rest was a miracle.

When Stella got home, it took her some time to wrap her mind around the fact that she was not alone. She actually had a family to which she belonged. Luigi said she had a home in Rome anytime she wanted to come for a visit or to live permanently. Stella promised to return and invited Luigi to visit her. Although her mother was gone, she was comforted by the revelation that her father was alive and well. Luigi gave her a copy of a picture of him and her mother, Grace. Stella had it framed and set it on her nightstand so that it was the first thing she saw in the morning and the last thing she saw before she fell asleep. It brought her such comfort and peace.

When Stella returned to work in her uncle's bookstore, she knew why she had felt so at home there.

She traveled back to Rome at least twice a year to spend time with her father and his family. She was always so surprised by the amount of love she was given, but she realized it was because of how much her father's family loved him. Since he never married and never had other children, Stella was the recipient of his legacy.

After working for two years in her Uncle Sal's bookstore, he sold it to Stella, although you couldn't actually call it a sale. He practically gave it to her. Sal always wanted to return to Rome, and selling the bookstore gave him the perfect opportunity to move back home permanently. While Stella missed him, she was elated that he trusted her with such a great part of his life. She transformed the quaint, nondescript bookstore into a hub of creativity—from book talks and speaker forums to political networking and local-art showcasing—while still maintaining its purpose of providing comfort and a sense of wonder through the printed word. Since Stella's Nook, as she renamed it, was privately owned, she could circumvent the political red tape imposed on venues that were supported by the local government. Anyone in the community who needed a job, a bondsman, a plumber, a tutor, a musician, a car, or a rare book could generally find it at Stella's Nook. Her bookstore became a mainstay of the community.

Word of the bookstore's popularity reached the local news station, and Stella was invited to anchor a weekly community-interest spot that grew into an hour-long program. From there, she was picked up by a national television station, and *Stella's Hour* was syndicated. She went from anchor to entertainer, finally putting her theater training to good use. First came live theatrical productions and then commercials and short films, and the rest was history.

Stella always found time to go on their biannual vacations with Charlotte, Florence, and Vivian. That was the one appointment that none of the girls were willing to miss—even if it meant that Charlotte had to coerce Bella into moving her wedding to November instead of June so that the vacation routine would not be interrupted.

CHAPTER 15

Never Too Late

"FLORENCE, WHEN DID you become so religious?" asked Stella one day when they were all sitting around on a rainy weekend and playing cards.

"She might be religious, but she sure is judgmental! And I know that is not a Christian virtue," added Vivian.

"And what would you know about Christianity, Vivian?" questioned Florence.

"Girl, I would have you know that I got my religion at the mourners' bench when I was ten years old. You must have forgotten that I am originally from the South, but don't tell anyone," laughed Vivian.

From her early childhood, Florence found solace in the church. Her first memories involved going there with her father, George. He was a deacon in the church, and as such, she spent a lot of time there. Florence's mother and siblings seldom attended, but the church provided time that Florence could spend with her father. After George died, Florence continued going because of her love for her father. As she got older, she developed a personal spiritual connection to God and the church. This faith shaped her outlook on life and influenced her relationships. Florence accepted the fact that she was far from perfect but practiced her faith seriously. Her one spiritual flaw was her tendency to judge others, and she knew it. That's because she was convinced that she was always right and anyone who did not agree with her way of thinking was wrong. She judged people's clothes, their music, their selection of friends, what they drank, what they did with their time, etc. She had an opinion on everything and scrutinized everyone's behavior. Sometimes she kept her opinions to herself, but more often than not, she felt it was her obligation to let people know their faults, such as telling Charlotte she was uppity sometimes and calling Vivian self-centered and reminding Stella that her taste in clothes advertised her as an exhibitionist. But many years would pass before Florence finally admitted to herself that a judging spirit did not conform to the teachings of Christ and when she passed judgment on others, she was unconsciously trying to usurp God's authority. Her prayer list always included a petition for deliverance from this sin because she thought it held up some of her blessings.

From the first day Florence started teaching, she poured herself into her craft, earning a reputation for being a caring teacher as well as an excellent leader. She exhibited a warm but commanding presence in the classroom and a supportive confidence toward the parents, and she demonstrated intolerance toward uncommitted colleagues. She basically lived and breathed every aspect of her profession. Her workday started at 7:30 a.m., and many nights, Florence would be up until 11:00 p.m., developing or editing lesson plans that encouraged self-confidence and enhanced student performance; she would do anything to bring out the best in her students. Her summers, when she was not vacationing with the girls, were spent attending workshops that deepened her knowledge of teaching methodology. She lived by the wisdom of "iron sharpened iron," meaning that you should surround yourself with people who can keep you sharp. Such intentional focus on her profession left little time for love and romance. Florence was always energetic with her students, playing ball, racing, and dancing. During a particular recess, Florence overheard some of her colleagues complimenting her on her rapport with the students.

"It's too bad that she doesn't have any. I don't know what she waiting for. If she wants to land a man and start a family, she needs to hurry. Those eggs have an expiration date, you know."

For the first time ever, Florence began to experience tumultuous feelings as she faced the fact that she was approaching a period in her life when the possibility of becoming an old maid was real. Maybe she was not a beauty queen like Stella, but Florence knew she had some desirable qualities: she was fashionable and had a good figure, was an accomplished educator, and was a consummate friend. Vivian and Charlotte were both married with children, and Stella didn't seem to care. But Florence always wanted a traditional family with a husband and children—in that order.

Moving along the road from birth to life's end, we find twists, turns, roadblocks, and detours. Each of us learns how to deal with these interruptions while at the same time finding a share of happiness. Florence wanted her share.

"I am a good person. I know I am not perfect. And I am trying to stop cussing and judging others. When will it be my turn? Where is my happiness? Or am I destined to live alone as punishment for my sin?" she often questioned.

Life's journey does not take everyone in the same direction because there are different lessons that we must learn along the way. But opportunities to find our bit of happiness often appear unexpectedly and briefly, and we need to be ready and willing to take a chance to move forward.

Florence was late for school this morning. Her alarm didn't go off as usual, but she usually woke up before the alarm. But not this morning. She couldn't find her keys. It took her fifteen minutes to find them and only after she asked the Holy Spirit for help. When she got in the car, the car was almost on empty—something that very seldom, if ever, happened to her. As she rounded the corner to head for the gas station, her car started slowing down. She was able to pull it to the curb before it finally stopped.

She had run out of gas.

All she could think about was her class of twenty-five first graders waiting for her, and she started to cry. After about five minutes, a car pulled up next to her, and Ronald Wilson jumped out.

"Good morning, Madam. Is everything all right?"

After Florence stopped wiping her eyes, she explained that her car had stopped and she didn't know why and she was late for work and her students would be left alone, and then she started crying again.

"Don't worry, Miss. Let me check it out," said Ronald.

After ten minutes, Ronald smiled and told Florence that she had just run out of gas.

~

"What? Out of gas? I can't believe it!" said Florence.

"I have a gas can in my car. Let me take care of it. I will be back shortly."

"Oh, thank you, Mister."

And with that, Ronald Wilson came to Florence's rescue, and she made it on time to her class of twenty-five students with five minutes to spare.

It was two weeks later that Florence ran into Ronald at the local farmers' market. She felt someone tap her on the shoulder. As she turned around, Ronald asked Florence if this was a better day for her. Florence replied that it was and thanked him again for coming to her rescue.

Their conversation lasted about an hour, and Florence learned a lot about her rescuer. Through discreet questioning, she found out all she needed to know: divorce for six years, not currently in a serious relationship, two children (a grown son in college and a fifteen-year-old daughter who was spending the summer with his parents, who lived two hours away), police officer, Christian, veteran, owns his own home, and has two sisters. His credentials met her requirements, but she wasn't thrilled about his being divorced with children, so Florence took his phone number and promised to call him.

When Florence got home, she replayed over and over in her mind her encounter with Ronald Wilson, and at the thought of him, her space was filled with peace.

Florence and Ronald had a standing date to go to the farmers' market every Saturday. They would then go to either Florence's apartment or his house and make breakfast with some of the produce they had bought. Ronald ended his breakfast with a fried apple pie that he always bought from the white-haired lady whose booth was situated near the door. As they passed her booth, he would flash her a big smile, hand her the exact change, and accept his pie, which was always ready for him. After he ate the pie with his coffee, he always ended his meal by saying, "This pie always tastes just like my grandma's."

After dating for four months, Ronald invited Florence to accompany him to pick up his daughter from his parents'. Florence was not comfortable with meeting his parents and was especially apprehensive about meeting his daughter, who was already a teenager. All the way there, Florence was uncharacteristically quiet, pretending that she was asleep. When they arrived at his parents' house, Ronald's daughter, Amy, was waiting on the porch, and she ran to the car; she hugged him as soon as he got out of the car. When she let go, Ronald introduced her to Florence, and she extended her hand and said "Hello, Ma'am" with a smile. Florence felt really good. Ronald led them into the house, not able to get a word in over the excitement of Amy's conversation. Ronald's parents were cordial; his father was inviting, but his mother was a bit more cautious and reserved. Florence could see her sizing her up.

His mother had lunch ready for them and the food was absolutely delicious. Florence could cook, but this was so much better. After lunch, Ronald's mother packed enough food for a month for Amy to take back before reminding Ronald to put some of it in the freezer. After Amy's bags were in the car, everyone said their goodbyes, but before they drove off, Ronald's mother said to Florence "I hope to see you again. Ronald is a good man. Just be patient" and smiled.

Two brief months later, Florence made the call to Charlotte, who almost dropped the phone.

"What? Getting married? When? Who is he?"

"Well, his name is Ronald Wilson, and we have been dating for about six months. I met him on the week after our vacation to Venice," explained Florence.

Florence explained that Ronald was a private person and so was she, so they spent a lot of time on getting to know each other before letting others know of the relationship.

"Well, when is the wedding?"

"In three months, in a church, and I am not having a maid of honor—just three bridesmaids. I know this seems to be quick, but my biological clock is ticking so loud, I can't sleep at night. It will be a small, private wedding—just family—and you all are my family. I am putting it off for three months because I know Stella will say that she needs time to diet," laughed Florence.

After a lengthy conversation with Charlotte, Florence called Vivian and Stella, and the date was set.

Charlotte got home after a twelve-hour shift in the OR and was about to fall onto her bed when she decided to play her telephone messages. The third call was from Stella. The volume of her answering machine was stuck on low, and the connection was a little muffled, but what she could hear from the message, she could hardly believe: "Marriage over . . . Florence leaving . . . meet me at Florence's . . . soon as possible. Already on the plane. Love you!"

Charlotte replayed the message and was able to make out a little more of it. This time, she heard Stella say that Ronald told Florence that their marriage was over. He would allow Florence to stay in his house only until the end of the month. They had only been married for eighteen months. "We have to go get her" was Stella's command.

Vivian, Stella, and Charlotte all arrived in Atlanta by 11:30 a.m. the next day. After the other girls were briefed by Stella, they went to Florence's house. Florence was there, but Ronald was at work and would not be home until 8:30 p.m. After crying, cussing, and screaming, a plan was made, and its execution was begun. By 3:30 p.m., an apartment had been leased, and a moving van had been contracted. By 7:30 p.m., everything that belonged to Florence had been packed up and loaded onto the moving truck. It would head for an apartment fifty miles away and was followed by a car carrying four angry women. Nothing of Florence's presence was left in that house—not even her scent. When they got to the new apartment, the movers unloaded the truck, brought everything into the apartment, and were gone by 11:30 p.m.

Exhausted, they got ready for bed. Vivian spread three quilts, four sheets, and two comforters on the carpeted floor and made a makeshift bed.

"You make a good bed, Vivian," said Charlotte.

"Once you have slept on a pallet, you never forget," smiled Vivian.

"And no, Florence, this does not count as one of our vacations. You still owe us," teased Stella.

And with that final word, they all laughed and went to sleep.

Four weeks after the moving incident, Florence called Charlotte in a panic.

"I'm late! So late! Charlotte, I'm late!" cried Florence.

"Late for what, girl?" asked Charlotte.

"I'm late! Don't you understand? I'm never late!"

"Oh—that kind of late. How late?"

"At least four weeks late. I did not notice until this morning. What am I going to do, Charlotte?" cried Florence.

"Hold on—I have tomorrow off, and I will be there as soon as possible."

Florence was forty-two, and she was indeed pregnant!

Charlotte and Vivian arrived at Florence's apartment to offer comfort and advice. They called Stella and put her on speakerphone. Vivian was curious as to how Ronald would react. "It is Ronald's, isn't it?" she teased before dodging the pillow Florence threw at her.

The consensus of the group was for Florence to call Ronald and find out where his head was. So she called him. She tried to put him on speakerphone, but Charlotte shot that down. She sent Florence into the other room and made coffee while they waited for Florence's report.

When Florence returned, she was smiling, and they called Stella again so she could hear the conversation. Florence told them that Ronald was excited about having a baby and being a new father. He wanted to come over this evening so they could discuss their future.

"Your future? Really, Florence?" Stella yelled through the phone.

The three friends thought that was not a good idea, and they told Florence how they felt. Was Rebecca still in the picture? Was she still coming to Sunday dinner at his mother's house? Does she still pick up his daughter from band practice? If the marriage ended because Ronald never ended his friendship with Rebecca, his former fiancée, which Florence made clear to Ronald was troubling to her, what made her think there would be a future for them? A baby should not shoulder the responsibility for keeping a marriage together. "You're grown," insisted Stella. "Florence, you have to handle your own business. Are you scared that you can't raise a child alone?"

Charlotte jumped in. "'Alone'? What are we, chopped liver? If it had not been for the three of you, Dawson and I never would have been able to raise Bella. I know I was never struggling for money, but with my mother being gone before I became a mother, I had no parenting skills. I would have let that sweet little girl run me out of my house and home when she was six or I would have been in jail for abandonment if it had not been for you all. You all know that child was a handful!"

They all shared a much-needed laugh.

Florence reconciled with Ronald, and they were determined to make their marriage work, especially after little Ashton was born. They took joint ownership for the care and nurturing of Ashton, and Florence turned into a great cook and housekeeper. Despite Ronald's responsibilities as a police officer and Florence's demands as an assistant principal, they were able to carve out time each month for a date night so the two of them could spend some adult time. Things went well during the honeymoon phase of their marriage. But after a few years, romance got crowded out by reality, and Ronald was having difficulty with adjusting to the normal expectations of marriage. Florence let her friends know to not expect her at all during their regular social gatherings because she was working on her marriage, but this was not so for Ronald.

He was still a little self-absorbed and persisted in involving himself in associations and social activities as he had as a single man, not understanding that in a marriage, some personal freedoms must be relinquished. Ronald just never adjusted to married life. He suffered from spur-of-the-moment syndrome. This quality was endearing while they were dating, but Florence now expected him to be more focused, more grounded, and more growth-oriented. And he continued his relationships with his single women friends. He didn't understand why Florence would have a problem with it. She knew he loved her and had no reason to be jealous. But jealousy was not the main issue. She expected a husband to take more interest in being with his family than being with his old friends. And Ronald thought Florence was not flexible enough and too closed-minded to understand his point of view. After about six years of marriage, Florence realized that she and Ronald were just not meant to be. She tried to force it but realized it was never going to work and they both deserved better. She didn't regret the marriage because of Ashton, but she and Ronald had two very different ideas about what *love* and *marriage* mean, and she knew they would never be able to reconcile those differences. They gave it the old college try but came to realize that a final dissolution of their marriage was inevitable, and they parted as friends.

CHAPTER 16

You Can Go Home Again

F LORENCE WAS BAKING cupcakes for Ashton's day-care class when the phone rang. When she answered the phone, she recognized the voice of her brother Jacob on the other end.

"Hey, Jacob. I haven't heard from you in two years. Is everything okay?" asked Florence.

"Not really. Mom is dead."

Florence was authentically sad. Although she never formed a warm and fuzzy bond with her mother like she did with her father, she did love her. Jacob told Florence that their mother had no life insurance and they all needed to help pay for the funeral. She had left specific instructions that stated that her body should be buried next to her parents in a cemetery over twenty-five miles from where her husband, George, was buried. Incidentally, it was the same cemetery where Deacon Ralph Milton was buried. Just saying. And of course Florence paid the major portion of her mother's funeral expenses.

Charlotte, Vivian, and Stella were there to support Florence at her mother's funeral. Even though all three of them had experienced the death of a loved one, they were mature enough to understand that each person's loss is unique to them. They were there to do and be whatever Florence needed. And they knew what she needed. After the funeral, they secured a babysitter for little Ashton, rented a luxury hotel suite, and brought out the playing cards, music, and ice cream and had an evening of grieving, sharing, comforting, and healing among friends.

Florence was feeling a little depressed after the death of her mother as it came on the heels of the death of her marriage. Oh how she missed her father. After her friends returned to their homes, Florence decided to drive the thirty-five miles to visit his grave site. Florence's faith taught her that George was not really in the cemetery, but whenever she stood where his body was buried, she got the feeling that he was still watching over her. Besides, she had never introduced Ashton to his grandfather. She did not want to overwhelm Ashton with thoughts of death since they had just come back from Eleanor's funeral, so she took extra time to prepare him for the cemetery visit. To help him not feel like just a spectator, Florence helped Ashton select a dwarf coreopsis to plant at his grandfather's headstone. When Florence and Ashton got to the final resting place of her father, they sat on the ground, and she started the conversation. It was very lighthearted because although Florence loved and missed her father, she never really grieved because she knew they loved each other unconditionally and she knew death was not final. She introduced Ashton to his grandfather and told him all about what a wonderful person his grandfather was—how he was a veteran and served his country during the war, what a great voice he had, how he sang with the choir at church, and how he loved her and always took care of her. Florence promised Ashton that she would always love him and watch over him the same way. As she was talking, she heard someone walk up to them, and after turning around, she saw a familiar face. It was Pastor Eric Robinson.

"I thought I heard your voice, Florence," said Pastor Robinson.

Florence ran to hug the pastor. Aston was a little scared to see his mother in tears, and he started to cry.

"Oh, honey, Mommy is fine. This is her good friend Pastor Robinson. And, Pastor, this is my son, Aston," said Florence.

Pastor Robinson was especially happy to see Florence and her son.

Florence explained that she just needed to feel close to her father today. She knew he was not really here, but she felt closer to him at his grave site than at any other place.

Rev. Robinson told Florence that he often visited his friend in the cemetery as well when he is in the area.

"When I visit with your father, he always ask me how his little girl is doing and I always say you are fine"., he said with a smile. "You are fine, aren't you, Florence?"

"I have been better," said Florence.

Pastor Robinson invited Florence and her son to accompany him to dinner and she accepted. They talked and talked, and Florence experienced such comfort and peace in a way that she had not known since her father died.

When Florence and Aston returned to Atlanta, she had regained her self-worth. She was so grateful to Pastor Robinson, and before they left, she invited him to visit them in Atlanta. She realized that she did not really consider him as a father figure and interestingly began to find him rather attractive. She discussed it with Vivian, who encouraged her to pursue a relationship with the reverend. After all, they had known each other for years, both were single, and Aston could use another male figure in his life.

After a six-month courtship, Florence became Mrs. Florence Spencer Robinson, first lady of the New Beginnings Missionary Baptist Church—a position for which she had been groomed for all her life.

CHAPTER 17

Affair or Relationship

THIS TIME, STELLA did not call Charlotte or Florence or Vivian when she returned from her out-of-town business trip. They would have to wait. Her mind was on Howard and how much she had missed him and how she was looking forward to being with him this weekend. Stella and Howard had been together for almost two years—one weekend at a time. Was it simply an affair or a genuine relationship? She was determined to find out which it was this weekend. Her friends had never met Howard, nor had she even mentioned his name in their presence. Why Stella was keeping him a secret from her friends, she didn't quite understand herself. She would call them after she had seen Howard and either fess up if it was a relationship or keep quiet if it was an affair.

Stella met Howard at the resort in Aruba where she and her friends were staying during one of their biannual vacations. Stella's luggage was misplaced by the airline, and she would have to go back to the airport the next day to retrieve it. It was a blessing that Florence or Vivian's luggage was not the one that went missing because if so, the entire vacation would have been a disaster. But Stella always kept her cool and never was the one to bring drama. Stella insisted on going back to the airport alone, insisting that the others just relax on the beach.

When she arrived at the terminal, she went to the lost-and-found counter and discovered she was not the only passenger with misplaced luggage. There were ten others in the same situation. Stella got in line and noticed a tall, handsome man in front of her. He turned around as she approached and gave her a once-over; he obviously liked what he saw because he smiled. Stella clearly liked what she saw for she smiled as well. After the young man got his luggage, he was rushed away by the driver of the shuttle that was taking him to a resort on the other side of the island but not before he shot one more long, piercing look at Stella that clearly showed his regret that there was not enough time to get acquainted with her. Stella's glance let him know that she understood and agreed with him as she was rushed in the opposite direction.

After their vacations were over and they returned to the airport to go home, it was coincidental that the handsome young man with the missing luggage was seated next to Stella on the return flight. By the time they landed, they had learned quite a bit about each other. He introduced himself as Howard A. Parker—account executive for a Fortune 500 company, single, no children, no siblings, both birth parents died in an automobile accident when he was seven, adopted by a distant relative to which he never bonded, independent, and career-driven. After Stella shared her story, they realized that they had a lot in common. As the plane was preparing to land, they discovered that they would both be in Chicago in two months and made a date to meet. Ever since then, like clockwork, they met every two months. Neither one of them was looking for a permanent relationship as each wanted to concentrate on their respective careers. They just enjoyed their time together—no strings. This relationship—or affair—had lasted for well over a year. How she kept the girls from finding out about him, Stella did not know herself because they shared everything, especially if something related to men. She couldn't explain why she kept this part of her life secret from her best friends.

On their two-year anniversary, they made plans to meet at a mountain resort. Howard had called ahead to make sure their room was stocked with all the things he knew Stella liked: crusty French baguettes with goat cheese, blueberry cheesecake, beautiful lavender orchids, and smooth jazz.

Stella arrived about an hour before Howard and couldn't help but smile at his thoughtfulness. She had mentioned only once that lavender orchids were her favorite, and Howard remembered. By the time Howard arrived, Stella had eaten most of the bread and cheese and was feeling relaxed from the chardonnay. She was lucky to have met such an attentive and caring man. When he walked into the room, his presence filled her with such contentment that she was almost startled. Maybe she did want this on a more permanent basis. Howard cautioned Stella not to eat any more bread and cheese because he had made reservations for dinner and dancing, if she was up to it. The restaurant was more of a bar that served steak and potatoes but had a large dancing floor. Stella loved to dance, and she discovered that Howard not only enjoyed dancing but was excellent at it. From the first time they danced together, their bodies moved in sync, his body muscular and graceful and hers relaxed and fluid as he led her body across the floor. Yes, she had to finally admit to herself as they were dancing cheek to cheek that she was in love with Howard. When they returned to the suite after such a romantic evening and finished the last of the chardonnay, Howard told Stella that they needed to have a serious conversation about their future—*their future*. Howard confessed that his thoughts of the future included Stella, and he wanted to know how she felt.

Stella asked, "Are you proposing to me?"

Howard smiled and, after a little hesitation, said he needed Stella to know something first before he asked her that. He went on to tell her that he always wanted to have children—to be a father—but due to a childhood injury, it was apparently impossible. He accepted the fact that the circumstances were beyond his control, but he really wanted to be a father. So he made up his mind and found an alternative way to become a parent. Two years ago, shortly before they met, he had started procedures to become an adoptive parent. He was acutely aware that there were so many children just like he was who, for no reason of their own, were without families who loved them. He wanted to provide that love. The adoption agency contacted him two days ago and said his application had been approved and they had an older child whom they thought would be a perfect fit. He had to give them an answer as soon as possible.

He had no idea when he began the adoption process that he would find someone like Stella, who had stolen his heart, and he knew this was information that might have been too much for her at this time. But he wanted to know how Stella felt about having children, becoming a mother, and adoption in general. Stella was about to answer him, but he stopped her and asked her to take two weeks to think about it since it was such a life-altering proposition and let him know her true feelings afterward. He insisted that they not discuss it anymore and said that after the two weeks were over, she should just give him a call. He kissed her and left.

After they headed home, Stella realized that she did need to think long and hard about what Howard was presenting and should be absolutely certain of whatever answer she would give. She was sorry that Howard couldn't physically father children, but adoption was an excellent choice and something she would definitely be open to. Stella had always been something of an activist, and she knew there were many children who needed homes—just like she did after her mother died with no idea of who her father was. She had many issues with Jean, but she was grateful that she didn't end up in one foster home after another. She took the two weeks and really counted up the cost of what an affirmative answer would mean. She finally made her decision.

Howard arranged to meet Stella for dinner after the two weeks were over. After they were served beverages, Stella told Howard that she had given the idea a lot of thought and prayer, and the idea of raising a family with him was one that she would be honored and blessed to be able to do. She knew he was a good man and would make a great father, so her answer was yes. Then Howard got on one knee in the restaurant, retrieved a simple but elegant diamond ring with a 0.92 carat solitaire set in 14K white gold from his pocket, and asked Stella to marry him. And, of course, she said, "Yes! Definitely yes!"

On the drive home, Stella started turning over in her mind how she would tell her best friends that she was getting married to a man they had never met or had even heard of and why she had kept her relationship with him secret from them. Stella still wasn't sure herself. She did know that she did not want an elaborate wedding as Vivian and Charlotte had—just a small, intimate ceremony with close friends. She couldn't wait to tell the girls. The excitement of getting married was slowly creeping up her back. She was also excited that in two weeks, she and Howard would be meeting with an adoption agency to get approval for their child.

Stella called her friends and invited them up for the weekend. She told them she had something important to share with them and they just had to come. Not wanting to be left out, all three women made it to Stella's. When they got there, they patiently ate the great brunch Stella had prepared, but Florence couldn't wait to hear the news.

"Well, Stella, what is so important that I had to leave town on the weekend of the annual 65 percent shoe sale? And you know how I like shoes—especially if they are on sale," said Florence. "And the plane ticket depleted my vacation account."

"Before we get started, Stella, pass me another one of your—" Vivian stopped midsentence and screamed. "Stella! What is that on your hand? It looks like an engagement ring! It is, isn't it?" Vivian screamed again.

"Yes, that's my news. I am getting married in two months. It will happen in Atlanta because that's where we will be living, and I want you all to be there," said Stella.

"Getting married! To who or to what! I didn't even know you were dating anyone!"

"Who is he? What is his name? Where is he from? Do you have a picture? Where does he work? Does he have a job?"

The questions kept coming, but Stella asked them to hold on and told them she would answer all their questions in time. Stella proceeded to share Howard with them—how they met, how long they were together, and when and where they met over the years. But the question of why she kept him a secret, she could not answer.

After about an hour of sitting on the hot seat, Stella had almost satisfied her friends' curiosity about the man who had stolen their friend's heart. Stella then called Howard and had him speak to each of her friends individually, and he answered all the questions they threw at him. After Howard hung up and everyone was satisfied with the answers, there was unanimous approval of Howard. There was still some hurt directed at Stella for keeping Howard in the shadows.

Two months later, Stella married the man of her dreams while she was surrounded by her very best friends. While Charlotte's and Vivian's weddings were elegant, classic, and large, Stella opted for simple and intimate. She wore a white lace sheath gown with a chapel train. It had thin straps and a neckline that highlighted a décolletage that was low enough to make Howard dream of things to come but high enough to not offend Rev. Robinson, who was the officiator. Since the dress was simple, she styled her hair with a gorgeous four-inch ivory-colored enamel hair accessory that depicted a butterfly sitting on frosted leaves and sparkling rhinestones, a gift from her father Luigi. To complete the feminine concept, Stella carried a bridal bouquet of warm blush-toned wildflowers accented with miniature white gardenia blossoms and sprigs of green that radiated a fresh innocence that the occasion demanded. In the presence of her friends for life, Stella married Howard Anthony Parker.

"I still can't believe that heffa had that man stashed away this whole time. Howard is such a gem. Even his criminal background check came back clean," reported Florence.

"Criminal background? Florence, you didn't!" exclaimed Charlotte.

"Of course I didn't. Stella told me that she pulled it herself. She said Howard gave her permission to do so because he wanted her to be sure and he didn't want any secrets between them."

"I knew there was something about that man that I loved," said Charlotte.

Six months later, Stella called Vivian and told her she had another surprise.

"I can't stand another surprise from you, Stella. I don't think you can top the last one anyway. How is that man of yours?" said Vivian.

"He is great. But this surprise is just as wonderful," assured Stella.

"Well, don't keep me waiting," begged Vivian.

"Here goes—I am a mother now! I have a child!"

"I didn't think you were pregnant at the wedding! Girl, you must have carried that baby in your feet! Your stomach was so flat!" cried Vivian. "And aren't you too old to be having a baby anyway?" She then laughed.

"Hold on, Viv," said Stella. "Howard and I adopted a young boy. His name is Jason, and he is ten years old. Most adoptive parents look for a newborn, but we wanted to adopt an older child as they sometimes get stuck in the system. My child can grow up with everyone's children, and maybe one day, they can become best friends as we are."

Vivian was still full of questions, but she was so happy for Stella. They both talked and talked until Stella had to hang up so she could call Charlotte and Florence.

CHAPTER 18

First Saturday after Christmas

B Y THE TIME Christmas came around, everyone had been blessed with children. Charlotte had Isabella and Dawson Jr.; her sister, Barbara, had Nyla, Lenox, and Madison; Stella had Jason; Florence had Aston; and Vivian had Jennifer. Charlotte was hosting First Saturday, an annual Timmons family gathering that her mother started years ago, and the sounds of life that could be heard throughout her big house brought her such pleasure. The smells of the foods she prepared using her mother's recipes, especially the ones for gingerbread, impregnated the atmosphere with the aromas of the season and memories of good times and family. The food was supposed to be light, but with such good cooks who secretly tried to outdo each other, they had a feast. Vivian brought her mother's famous angel biscuits; Florence brought a ham and scalloped potatoes—the reverend's favorite; Stella brought panettone, which she learned to bake while living with her father in Italy; Barbara cooked pies—sweet potato, coconut, and pecan—which were testimonies of her southern heritage; and Charlotte supplied the vegetables and refreshments and, of course, the rainbow cake with seven-minute icing that her Grandmother Beulah insisted be present at every family gathering. At the sight of it, Charlotte and Barbara looked at each other and had a private moment. Everyone enjoyed the meal—even the children. Charlotte had made preparations to have the men retire to Dawson's attached workshop where they could watch all the football they wanted. She made sure they had enough drinks and food to keep them occupied for the whole day and even into the early evening. Florence was dying to go with the men because she really loved football. She especially missed her father during times like this, but she knew her place today was in the kitchen with the women and children, although she did volunteer to keep the men's food and drink replenished and check in with them at the beginning of each quarter.

"Stella, Jason is quite a handsome fellow. Do you know anything about his background?" asked Charlotte.

Stella explained that her little boy was living in an orphanage in Seattle when Howard saw him for the first time.

"You know Howard was adopted, and so was I, sort of, and he vowed that when he became an adult, he would get at least one child out of the system," she said.

She continued to explain that when he visited the orphanage, he saw Jason playing chess alone and struck up a conversation with him, and then he just knew that Jason was the one. They both fell in love with him immediately, and the rest was history.

"I am so happy to be a mother, Charlotte—so happy."

"I hope there are many great adoptive parents in this world like the two of you Stella", Charlotte said.

"I am sure there are", encouraged Stella.

CHAPTER 19

Lean on Me

S TELLA NEVER LIKED it when Howard worked late because food is never as good as it is when it is freshly prepared and not warmed over. But since he was not home by seven, she knew he would be really late. Stella was definitely tired and decided to take a lavender bath and go to bed. She was always a hard sleeper, but when she woke up, she had a strange feeling. The room was so quiet that she knew Howard was not there. She tried calling him again and again. There was no answer.

When the sun came up the next morning, Howard was still not home. Jason came into the room, looking for his father, which was his regular routine. Stella began to panic.

Then the phone rang. The caller was not her husband. With a heavy heart, the caller told Stella what she never wanted to hear.

Howard was in a terrible six-car pileup on the interstate. The taxi he was in was pinned under a tractor trailer. It took over two hours to get him free from the wreckage because his taxi had gone down a ravine. By the time Howard was rescued, he had lost a lot of blood and was unconscious. The medical professionals did all they could, but Howard never regained consciousness and unfortunately died. The wreckage involved multiple victims, and emergency personnel were only now able to identify the victims. Stella was distraught. The information was too much to process alone.

Lucky for her, she had a network of very good friends whom she relied on. Stella went through the funeral in a blur. Her friends took care of everything. They planned the service, notified all the friends and family, and took great care that Jason was comforted and not afraid. As soon as the funeral was over, Stella's father insisted that she and Jason come back with him to Italy for a few weeks. Those few weeks turned into six months and then six years. During that period of time, Stella's father died of an apparent heart attack. She was so grateful that she got the chance to get to know him and that Jason had time to benefit from bonding with his grandfather. After Luigi's death, Stella and Jason returned to the States to pick up where they left off.

CHAPTER 20

A Time for Self-Preservation

"HELLO, HONEY. WAIT! Hold on! Hold on!" Florence tried to calm Isabella down. "Tell me again slowly what you said."

Charlotte made an appointment to have a mammogram. She was not scheduled for another one for seven months, but while she was in the shower, she found a lump. As a nurse, she knew she needed to have it examined as soon as possible, and she was able to get an appointment that same afternoon. The doctor did a breast biopsy and scheduled her to return in two days. As soon as she got back home, she called Bella and explained what was going on. Charlotte hugged Bella and told her it was probably nothing and not to worry. She knew Bella had a recital in two weeks, and she wanted her to be ready. And she asked her not to tell DJ and Dawson because the men were no good in difficult situations and she just didn't want to worry them unnecessarily. Bella tried to keep up appearances and look like she was not worried, but she had always looked to her mother for strength, and she knew her mother needed it now. Bella drove her mother back to the doctor's office for her follow-up appointment to get the results. It was positive.

Bella and Charlotte rode in silence back home. Bella loved her mother, and there was nothing she wouldn't do for her at any time—day or night—but she knew her mother needed something that she could not give. She needed to remember who she was before this life-changing moment—before she was a wife and mother and before the weight of the world was placed on her heart. At this time, she needed to only be concerned about her health and her life, and only her best friends could do that. They started sharing this journey with her years before she had a husband and children. They would remind her of the tears, smiles, laughter, memories—all those things necessary to tap the reservoir of strength she would need to enter self-preservation mode. There would be plenty of time for her to return to putting Dawson and the children first, but this had to be Charlotte's time, and her friends would make sure of that. As soon as they returned home and opened the door, Florence, Vivian, and Stella were there, waiting for Charlotte with open arms.

CHAPTER 21

Tough Love

SINCE SHE WAS a young child, Jennifer had been difficult. She seemed to have been born with a rebellious spirit. Nothing serious—she just did not like taking directions from anyone—whether at home or in school. Vivian tried all the prevailing parenting tools over the years: spanking, time-out, grounding, taking away of privileges, taking a hands-off approach—everything she could think of, but nothing seemed to work for long. Herman Jr. was disinterested in any type of parental control, and Vivian was always the bad guy in their home. And, of course, Constance, her mother-in-law, did not help. Vivian was literally pushed aside when her child was born, and this had eroded her authority in the eyes of her family. Constance took charge of all the birthdays and took the child to the beach for weeks at a time during the summers and to ski lodges in the winters. She did all these things without getting permission or approval from Vivian or Herman Jr. The only person who would challenge his wife's interference was her husband, Herman Sr., but after a while, even he gave up. As a result, the child grew up with a severe entitlement complex. Jennifer learned that if she appeased her grandmother, she could get whatever she wanted. If Vivian ever objected to anything, Jennifer would run straight to Constance, who always took her side without hearing the whole story. When Jennifer turned fifteen, she was out of control. Being disrespectful, lying, manipulating, skipping school, smoking, and drinking were activities common to Jennifer. By the time she was seventeen, things between mother and daughter had become so toxic that Jennifer moved in with Constance without Vivian's blessings. To add salt to the wound, Constance even bought Jennifer a luxury car—again without consulting her parents. That situation lasted approximately five months until Constance began to see the real picture. Jennifer would stay out until the wee hours of the morning and invite all types of people inside Constance's house. She began asking for more and more money to finance the lifestyle to which she had become accustomed. After Jennifer wrecked the car for the third time and had received several driving violations, including DWIs, Constance was finally fed up. She made her park the car—since it was in her name—and sent her packing back to her parents. Constance swallowed her pride and called Vivian to apologize for interfering and taking Jennie's side and told her it wouldn't happen again. It had become obvious that Jennifer had intentionally been playing the two of them against each other to get her way.

When Jennifer returned to her parents' home, she said all the right words to make peace with her mother. She went to school on time, came home at a decent hour, and helped more around the house. She even got a part-time job. After a month of good behavior, Jennifer began sliding back into her old manipulative habits and tried to persuade Vivian to ask Constance to allow her to drive her car again. But Vivian knew her child and knew she had not changed. Vivian told Jennifer she would revisit the issue of the car in another month. This infuriated Jennifer. She called her grandmother and thanked her for being so patient with her and allowing her to stay at her house. Jennifer knew her grandmother was a pushover for flattery and said all the right words and did all the right things so that with only a little nudging, she convinced Constance that she had become a more mature and responsible person. As a sign of her new sense of responsibility, Jennifer suggested that since she had a job, she could be accountable for the upkeep of the car, and she asked her grandmother if she would transfer the car title and the insurance to her. Jennifer's words convinced Constance that it was a good idea and a sign that Jennifer had indeed changed. When the title of the car came with Jennifer's name on it, she was pleased with her handiwork. When she told her mother what her grandmother had done, Vivian was upset—primarily with Constance because she again had not consulted with Jennifer's parents before making decisions that could have major consequences. Jennifer assumed that since the car was now in her name, she did not need her mother's permission to drive.

After all, it was really her car now. But Jennifer assured her mother that she would wait for her approval. Vivian had to admit that Jennifer's attitude had improved a little, but she was still involved with the same group of unsavory friends that continued to be in some kind of trouble or another. She told Jennifer that she had two more weeks left before she would revisit the idea of giving her permission to drive—whether the car was in her name or not. Just two more weeks—but two weeks were just too long for Jennifer. That evening, she sneaked out of her bedroom window, had one of her friends drive her to Constance's house, opened the garage with a key that Constance had forgotten to take back, and drove away with the car. The following morning, Vivian discovered that Jennifer was gone. She called Constance, and Constance checked the garage and verified that the car was indeed gone. They both knew that Jennifer had run away.

Vivian straightaway called the police, and they found her daughter two days later and brought her home. Jennifer ran away two more times before her eighteenth birthday.

An eighteenth birthday officially marks the end of childhood, at least legally, and no one was more ready for this day than Jennifer. During the three weeks leading up to her birthday, Jennifer was uncharacteristically sweet, respectful, attentive, and appreciative. Constance decided, with Vivian's permission, to plan a birthday pool party for her Jennie.

"Everyone needs an eighteenth-birthday party, and Jennie has been really good. Is it all right?" asked Constance.

Since Constance asked for permission, Vivian relented.

Constance invited all of Jennifer's friends, hired a great band, and had all her favorite foods catered. Constance always knew how to throw a great party. Everyone seemed to really enjoy the party, especially Jennifer. Even Vivian felt better about it. *Maybe it will be the beginning of a new attitude for Jennifer,* she thought.

The morning after her party, Jennifer packed her bags and walked out of her parents' house this time through the front door and not out of the window without even a goodbye or a glance backward. Vivian followed behind her and tried to persuade her to reconsider, but Jennifer made it clear that she was not interested in ever living with her family again. She wanted to live her life on her own terms without any interference, and she could now do so since she was a legal adult. After almost a year of calling, crying, and pleading with her daughter, Vivian stopped. Years passed before Vivian saw or heard from her little girl again. Until today.

Vivian decided to drive to the market to get some fresh eggs, garden vegetables, and strawberries. She had been dieting for two weeks, and she wanted to reward herself. Charlotte was always reminding her that if she didn't take care of herself, nobody else would. And today, she felt like she mattered, and she wanted cake and fresh strawberries. As she turned the corner, she saw a young girl who looked familiar. For a split second, she thought it looked like her baby girl, although Vivian knew that her fashion-conscious daughter would never have been caught dead in such clothing. But as she continued looking, she noticed that the young girl had the same walk as Jennifer. She was accompanied by an older man who looked just as unkempt as she was. Vivian slowed her car to get a better look. The girl had a hoodie that covered her hair and most of her face, but there was no mistaking the figure or the gait as that of her sweet daughter. Once Vivian made sure she was not mistaken, her first impulse was to stop the car, jump out, and take Jennifer home. But her head—her head knew she could not. She gripped the stirring wheel, looked straight ahead, and sped away toward home, crying all the way.

Two years later, there was a knock on the door one evening around 10:45 p.m. Herman was not at home as usual, and Vivian was a little afraid to answer the door. She quietly retrieved the pistol from her nightstand and, with gun in hand, approached the door and asked who it was.

"Mommy, it's me, Jennifer. Can I come in?"

Vivian hesitated for a few minutes, but her motherly love took over, and she opened the door to face her long-lost daughter. Jennifer practically fell into the room, looking quite emaciated, unkempt, and lost.

"I don't have anywhere to go. Can I please stay, Mommy?"

CHAPTER 22

Secrets Revealed

CHARLOTTE HAD JUST completed an emotional and physically demanding shift in the emergency room. The last of the eight trauma patients brought in from the warehouse explosion was finally stabilized and transferred to a room on the floor. Charlotte had been on her feet for a solid six hours, so as soon as she got home, she felt like falling into bed with all her clothes on. Dawson was at a medical conference, so Charlotte grabbed a bite of whatever was left in the refrigerator and headed for the shower. The phone rang, and it was Dawson. He was just checking to make sure Charlotte had gotten home and to say he loved and missed her. Feeling wonderful after Dawson's call, Charlotte realized that she had it good. She had a great husband who loved her and whom she loved and two wonderful children. Still warm because of Dawson's words, she checked all the locks to make sure the house was secure and headed once again for the shower even though it was only 8:00 p.m. Her phone rang again, but this time, it was not Dawson's voice on the other end.

"Good evening. I hope it is not too late, but this is Walter Nicholson. May I speak to Charlotte Timmons, I mean Charlotte Timmons Wright, please?"

"Walter Nicholson! I haven't heard from you in over twenty years! How are you?" asked Charlotte.

"Hey, Charlotte. You sound the same."

"And so do you, Walter. Where are you, and how did you find me here in Birmingham?"

"Charlotte, listen—I know it is late, but I just flew in and really need to talk with you. May I come by? I won't be long. This is really important," asked Walter.

"Sure, Walter. I hope everything is okay. And it is never too late to see an old friend," said Charlotte.

"See you in about thirty minutes. Thanks, Charlotte."

Charlotte couldn't imagine why Walter needed to see her now. Her mind went back to her time in Colorado but was sure Walter knew nothing about it. Maybe it had something to do with his family or his health. She quickly took that shower and changed into something comfortable. While waiting for Walter, she tried to imagine what could be so urgent. She didn't have to wait long because in about thirty minutes, Walter was ringing her doorbell.

"Walter Nicholson, it is so good to see you," began Charlotte as they surveyed each other before embracing in a long-overdue hug.

Charlotte invited Walter in and led him to the living room, where she had prepared a light snack of baked brie with figs and walnuts and a bottle of pinot noir. Walter exchanged pleasantries with her before bluntly asking, "Charlotte, do you and I have a child together?" He just blurted it out.

"A child? Why would you ask such a question, Walter?"

Walter then explained that two days ago, he received a phone call from an adoption agency; a young man who was surrendered to them when he was an infant was looking for his birth parents. The young man was to be married in six months and wanted to update his medical history so he would be aware of any health concerns.

"The agency said Water Nicholson and Charlotte Timmons are listed as his birth parents, and they wanted me to know before the information was released. Do you know anything about this? I know what a stickler you are for telling the truth, and I need to know."

Charlotte poured herself a drink and one for Walter also. "Where do I begin?"

Charlotte asked Walter if he could remember when he came by her house after her mother's funeral to console her and to make sure she wouldn't be alone.

"Well, it worked because in nine months, I had a baby," announced Charlotte.

"But why didn't you tell me? I had a right to know," said Walter.

Charlotte asked Walter to remember the last time they saw each other. In that restaurant in Chicago, she was about to tell him about the pregnancy, but before she could tell him, he jumped in and announced he was engaged.

"I was prepared to tell you I was pregnant, but after you said you were in love and getting married, I did not want to ruin your life, so I kept quiet," confessed Charlotte.

She explained that she made the decision to go away, have the baby, and pray that he was placed in a home with good parents. She wasn't prepared to raise a child alone, especially with her mother gone. When the agency gave her the adoption papers, she realized that the both of them were complicit in their reckless behavior, but the child had no say in the matter. She decided that if one day, the child needed to know something about his birth parents, she would remove any blocks.

"That's why I put the names of both birth parents on the adoption papers. I intended to tell you many times. I wrote you many letters but lost my nerve before I mailed them. I have never told anyone about us— not even my best friends. It is the one thing that has kept me awake on many nights during these last twenty-five years," confessed Charlotte.

"I do understand that you were in a hard place, but that is no excuse. You still should have told me, Charlotte. I had a right to know."

"I am so very sorry, Walter. Where do we go from here?"

"My wife and I never had children. She never wanted them, but I didn't find that out until after five years of marriage. We did try several times but to no avail. I think the idea of being pregnant was just too stressful for Peggy. She couldn't seem to carry one to term. I think it was partially responsible for our divorce. She ended the marriage, not me," confessed Walter.

"I didn't know you were divorced. How long?"

"Ten years. I always wanted children, and when I found out I had a child out there somewhere—well, I thought it was a miracle. I want to find him, but I want to know what you think about it first. Your secret will get out."

CHAPTER 23

Miracles Do Happen

STELLA WAS ALWAYS happy when she received a letter from her son. Phone calls were very much appreciated, but a letter written in his own handwriting was priceless. Stella was initially sad when Jason told her he wanted to go to college in Italy because she would miss him terribly, but she was really happy that he felt comfortable with his Italian family. It seemed that it was only yesterday that she drove him to the airport and sent him off with her blessings, reminding him to not forget to write.

"Mother, no one writes anymore. I will just call every once in a while," Jason reminded her.

"If Howard could see his son now, he would be so proud," thought Stella aloud.

After Jason moved to Europe without her, Stella was a little apprehensive, but she remembered when she moved all the way to Hollywood, California, and she didn't know anyone except that loser Sam. *But I guess I was the loser,* thought Stella, *since I almost let Sam cheat me out of my last $1,000 and stay at my apartment for almost a year rent-free.* But Jason wanted to be a philosopher—a *philosopher.* As for why, Stella had no idea. She tried to get him interested in medicine, mathematics, sports medicine, computers, and even the theater— anything that would keep him near her, but she let him go. *Everyone must travel their own path,* she thought.

Four years had passed quickly, and she was heading to Oxford University for his graduation. Only Charlotte was available to accompany her to England for Jason's graduation even though Stella offered to pay for everyone's transportation. Vivian was preoccupied with Jennifer's recovery, and Florence was the keynote speaker of her church's annual conference. Since she became First Lady Robinson, Florence had really blossomed. She even authored a guidebook on how to become an effective first lady. Who would have thought! When Isabella found out that Auntie Florence and Auntie Vivian could not travel with Auntie Stella, she begged her mother to let her come along. She argued that she and Jason were the closest of the "cousins" even though they were four years apart, and since she wanted to backpack through Europe the following year, Jason could show her around before she went on her own—all the things a mother of a soon-to-be eighteen-year-old high school graduate wanted to hear.

All the "cousins" knew how to get their way. They used a strategy called divide and conquer. Bella got Auntie Stella alone and asked her if it would be all right for her to come along. She said she really missed Jason and would love to see him in his graduation gown, and she thought he might be able to help her get into Oxford. Bella said she could pay her own way because she had been saving her money for the last four years to get a car, but she would much rather use it to see her favorite "cousin." "If it's okay, can you speak with my mother?" How could Stella say no? Within two days, Stella had convinced Charlotte and Dawson to let Bella come with them.

"Thank you, Auntie Stella! You were always the cool one!" said Bella with a wink and a smile.

Stella, Charlotte, and Isabella arrived on time at the Sheldonian Theatre for the graduation ceremony of the University of Oxford, and like any mother, Stella made sure Jason was wearing the appropriate dress underneath his full academic regalia. She was a proud mama. Several cousins of her Italian family came to celebrate Jason's accomplishments. After the ceremonies were over, Jason took Bella on a tour of the university and other spots of interest to young people. Stella and Charlotte were sure they were enjoying sights for which parents would not have the same appreciation. Charlotte trusted Jason to take care of Bella while she and Stella toured the Botanic Garden, visited the covered market, went in and out of every bookstore they passed, and ate cake from a pub as they leisurely walked along the River Thames.

Jason had told his mother months ago that he had decided to stay in Europe for at least two more years before returning to the States. He wanted to get a master's degree before leaving Europe. He had already secured a teaching-assistant position that would pay him enough to support himself. Bella asked her mother if she could stay in Europe with Jason for one year before beginning college. Charlotte's answer was an emphatic "No." No discussion. Bella knew when to leave something alone. This was one of those times.

When they returned home, Bella was still excited about her trip and wanted to live the life that her "cousin" Jason had. Charlotte convinced her to complete her undergraduate education in the States; if she could do that, then maybe she would consider letting her take her graduate studies abroad. Bella stopped complaining after two weeks when she discovered that the new student-body president at her college finally noticed her.

This last letter that Stella received from Jason was a little strange. He started out by stating his undying love for her. Stella and Jason had a very strong bond as mother and son. He didn't have to tell her that he loved her. She always knew. Then he talked a little about his father and how he was so blessed to have been rescued from a life of loneliness. As she continued to read, Stella began to get it. Jason, as most adoptees do at some point in their lives, wanted to find his birth parents. Stella knew this day would come, and as much as she thought she would be prepared for it, she was not. Jason was not looking for a reunification with his birth parents; he only wanted to know if there were any potential health issues in his family history that he should be concerned about. He didn't even need names—just health histories. He asked his mother if she would be willing to help him find his birth parents. Stella had no problem with it.

Jason's letter also mentioned that he was coming home in two weeks and was bringing a young lady with him so she could meet his mother. Jason was in love. He was thinking of marriage. That's why he was interested in his family health history. Who was the young woman who had stolen her son's heart? Stella knew the day would come when she would no longer be the number one woman in her son's life. When

Jason got off the plane, he was accompanied by a young woman who was about his height. She walked a little behind him but not with an attitude of submission but with one of respect. After greeting his mother, Jason introduced his friend, Ms. Abigail Richardson, to her. Stella sized up her replacement—not with a spirit of resentment but with one of curiosity. Abigail knew how to be polite, to not be overbearing, and to let Stella have all the time she needed with her son. When they got home, Stella made it clear with a smile—but in no uncertain terms—that Jason and Abigail would sleep in separate rooms.

Stella had prepared all of Jason's favorite foods: a simple garden salad without cucumbers, cheeseburgers, steak fries, a mozzarella and tomato pizza, and of course, gelato. Jason's favorite flavor was pistachio. Stella preferred the hazelnut-and-cinnamon flavor of biscotti gelato, and the go-to flavor of stracciatella was always in Stella's refrigerator.

Abigail thanked Stella for her hospitality and retired early so that mother and son could have their privacy. After eating the last of his gelato, Jason asked Stella what she thought of Abby.

"Why does that matter?" asked Stella.

Jason confessed that he was in love with Abby and he wanted to ask her to marry him. He had a great job and could support himself and a wife, and the only thing standing in the way of his asking her to be his wife was the absence of his family health history. He wanted to assure Stella that the need to locate his birth parents had nothing to do with the love he had for her and for his father, Howard.

Abigail stayed for two weeks, and Stella really began to like her. They went shopping together, and Stella even let her cook. She noted that Abigail—or "Abby," as she began to call her—was a really good cook, and she seemed to certainly love and respect Jason. *Maybe a daughter wouldn't have been so bad,* thought Stella. By the time Abby flew back to England, Stella had given Jason her approval. As soon as Abby boarded the plane, Stella and Jason went to work on looking for his birth parents.

They started with the orphanage where Howard first saw Jason. From there, they were led to the hospital where Jason was born. To their surprise, it was not in Seattle, Washington.

"Is it Arizona?" asked Stella.

"Why Arizona, Mother?" asked Jason.

"No reason," said Stella. She was comforted that it was not in Arizona.

It was Colorado. Jason had been adopted at the age of six months into a family in Colorado, but when he was two years old, they moved to Seattle, Washington. The family was dissolved by divorce when Jason was five, and both parents surrendered him to the welfare system and released him for adoption. Jason was sent to an orphanage and remained there until Howard found him. Jason had very few memories of his first adoptive family, and none of them were happy.

Stella and Jason identified the hospital where he was born and where his birth mother first surrendered him. Two weeks of telephone conversations convinced Stella that they needed to fly to Colorado and speak with those in authority face-to-face. After meeting some resistance, they finally got a copy of the coveted birth certificate and the surrender documents. Instead of tearing into the documents immediately, Jason decided not to open them until they got back home. He told his mother that he needed time to meditate to make sure he wanted to know what the documents would reveal about him. Stella couldn't believe he had the patience to wait—a trait he certainly did not inherit from her—but she honored his decision.

When they returned home and were seated at their table, Jason announced that he was ready to examine his birth documents. He insisted that they read them together. When they got to the names of the parents, they were speechless. There it was in black and white: "Mother: Charlotte Timmons; Father: Walter Nicholson."

After reading and rereading the documents, Stella placed a call to Charlotte. She was her old bubbly self and never hinted about what she had discovered, and after some small talk, she told her that since Jason was home, they decided to do a road trip in her direction and wanted to stop by if it was a good time.

"Good time? When did it ever have to be a good time to visit with family? Bella and DJ will be so excited to see Jason. Hurry up and get here," said Charlotte.

When Stella and Jason arrived, Charlotte, Dawson, Bella, and DJ were all standing on the front porch, waiting to get their first glimpse of Jason. It had been over three years since they had seen him. He had to embrace them all but was a little insecure in his embrace of "Auntie Charlotte." Charlotte had prepared a great brunch, and everyone got caught up on what had been happening in each of their lives since they last were together. After brunch, Dawson went to work, and Bella and DJ had obligations, but they begged Jason to stay until they returned. He promised that he would. After they were alone, Stella, Jason, and Charlotte moved to the sunroom to continue their visit.

Stella began talking. She told Charlotte all about Jason's girlfriend, Abby, and how much she and Jason were in love. Stella teased Jason that she had to stay one step in front of them to make sure they did not sneak into each other's room at night. They all had a good laugh.

The conversation topic changed to Jason's adoption. He explained that he wanted to find his birth parents because he wanted to ask Abby to marry him, but he was unsure of his health history. He was not necessarily trying to connect with them; he only wanted to know if there was anything in their health histories that he needed to be concerned about.

"I think that is a really responsible thing for you to do, Jason, You must really love Abby. I can't wait to meet her," said Charlotte.

"Thanks," said Jason. Then he continued to explain to Charlotte how he and his mother started the search, which took them to Seattle and then to Colorado, where he was actually born. At the mention of *Colorado*, the smile on Charlotte's face seemed to change to an expression of fear.

"As you know, my mother is relentless, and we were able to get the actual birth certificate. I brought it with me and thought you would be interested in seeing it, Auntie Charlotte," said Jason, and then he handed it to Charlotte.

"The interesting thing about it, Charlotte," said Stella, "is that you are listed as the mother and Walter is listed as the father. And I know it is your signature because I know you always put two marks across your *t*'s. So I guess my son is also your son."

And with that, Charlotte fainted.

When she came to, the three of them talked for almost two hours. Jason excused himself to call Abby. While he was gone, Charlotte asked Stella if she already knew. Stella assured Charlotte that she would have told her earlier if she knew. Stella reminded Charlotte that Colorado is a long way from Arizona. They then had a side discussion about how they both felt about being the mother of the same child. It was too much. They decided to table that conversation for another time.

Then Charlotte called Walter. He was so excited, he almost lost his breath. Then he insisted on talking with Jason and ended the conversation by stating that he was leaving immediately and would be there in four hours.

Charlotte summoned her husband and children home immediately to talk with them. When Walter arrived, they all seemed somewhat stunned and sat down to process the information. Dawson Sr., Dawson Jr., Isabella, Stella, Jason, and Walter were inundated with questions that only Charlotte could answer. She insisted that everyone feel free to ask any questions they might have about anything. Nothing was off the table.

CHAPTER 24

Pressure Over Time

FROM HER CHILDHOOD to events in college to her marriage and family, Vivian had learned to avoid the realities of life by pretending that she lived in an alternate universe. It helped her avoid unbearable hurt. But today, everything caught up with her. Vivian had a stroke. All that stress from living a lie, pretending that Herman was the perfect husband, and having to keep up the facade that her lazy, ungrateful child was loving, grateful, and successful had finally pushed Vivian over the edge. If only she could have just been honest with herself beginning with that elaborate wedding—no, going all the way back to that fairytale marriage proposal. The grapevine reported, by way of Vivian's mother, that Vivian actually proposed to Herman, and when he said he wasn't ready, Vivian told him she was pregnant. She even told his mother, who then insisted that they marry as soon as possible. Constance Washington III did not want a scandal in her nouveau riche family. She had plans for a political career for her husband. But Vivian was not pregnant, had never been pregnant, and lied that she had miscarried. Herman found out, but by then, it was too late. He never did stop seeing Patricia, his high school sweetheart.

On the morning of Vivian's stroke, Margaret, her housekeeper of twelve years, was curious that Vivian was still seated at the breakfast table when she arrived. She was prepared to listen to another account of how wonderful Herman was last night or how much Jennifer had begged her to come spend two weeks with her. Her "Morning, Mrs. Washington" was not answered with the usual "Glorious morning, Margaret" but with a weak and slurred "Marg."

"You all right, Vivian?" asked Margaret.

When Vivian made no reply, Margaret knew that something was wrong. She could see that the right side of Vivian's face was drooping, and her speech was slurred. She immediately dialed 911. And then she called Stella—even before calling Vivian's husband or her moneygrubbing, good-for-nothing daughter because she knew who would drop everything and meet her at the hospital.

Stella was there before the ambulance arrived. While waiting for a diagnosis from the emergency-room doctor, Stella called Charlotte, Florence, and then Herman. After about forty-five minutes, Herman finally arrived, looking agitated. Stella was in no mood to make small talk with him. She didn't like him, and she knew he knew she didn't ever since she saw him having dinner with Patricia at Vivian's favorite restaurant. But she was cordial for Vivian's sake and pretended that she thought Herman's concern was genuine. After fifty-five minutes had passed, the ER doctor came out with a diagnosis. Vivian had suffered a mild stroke, but since she got to the hospital in time, there would be only minimal damage. Stella updated Charlotte and Florence, and they made plans to come as soon as possible.

Charlotte stopped by a drugstore so she could fill all her prescriptions before heading for the airport. She had no idea how long she would be gone. Dawson had instructions to feed Joe Joe and Tiny and pay the gardener and housekeeper. He seemed to be so absentminded lately, and she didn't want to return and find her rose garden in disarray.

She could still hear the caution in Stella's voice. "I know it was Herman's fault—and that moneygrubbing daughter. She hasn't even shown up. Vivian should just face reality and dump that poor excuse of a family. If only she was not so vain and pretentious!"

Charlotte agreed with her. Vivian wanted so much to have the perfect life that through the years, she invented fairy tales to cope. She built a make-believe world, and that was what she ended up with—make-believe. Oh yes, she always had the money, nice cars, beautiful house, and fashionable clothes, but you could tell that her soul was famished. She possessed so much but got so little.

"Hey, Stella. How is Viv?"

"The doctor just left, and he said she will be fine—just a minor stroke, but Viv will have to rest and eliminate that stress."

"Where is Herman?"

"Herman is in there with Vivian. Eliminate stress! I think her family is the main cause of her stress!"

"Don't blame it all on Herman. You know Viv. She just needs to face reality."

"Oh Lord, here comes Florence. Head her off before she sees Herman."

"Where the hell is that no-good Herman and that daughter? I guess they will only be satisfied after Viv is dead!"

"Hold on, Florence," cautioned Charlotte. "This is not the time for drama. Let Vivian have some peace and quiet. Let her recover, and then you can lay into Herman. He is with Vivian now, Jennifer hasn't arrived yet. I guess she is waiting for Vivian to send her a plane ticket."

"You all are so hard on Jennifer. She is the way she is because of Constance and, yes, even Vivian. You know she was spoiled from the womb."

"Stella, you are always trying to defend that rotten family of Vivian's. She may have spoiled Jennifer, but she is an adult now, and should know better" was Florence's response.

Jennifer came up the hallway just as Florence finished her sentence.

"Hello, Aunties. Glorious day, isn't it?" Jennifer greeted them with her signature smile and in the language of her mother. "How is Mommy? She is so dramatic! She'll do anything to make me come back to this miserable town." Even after all those years of being clean, Jennifer was still as self-centered as ever.

Florence was the first to speak. "Your mother had a stroke. Margaret got her to the hospital in time, so there should be no major damage. I am sure you are anxious to see her, so you can go right in."

Jennifer tried to protest, but Florence gently but firmly led her to Vivian's room, opened the door, and nearly shoved her in. After returning to the other "Aunties," they could see Florence was about to blow her top. Charlotte and Stella almost lost it with laughter as they recounted to Florence how she totally ignored Jennifer's reluctance to rush into Vivian's room. Although Vivian had the best medical care, the girls insisted that Jennifer spend the night with her mother to make sure she didn't feel alone and to be there to hear the doctor's orders concerning Vivian's care once she was discharged. She would need a little help for a few months with bathing, getting dressed, and meal preparation.

"Vivian should be able to come home from the hospital tomorrow, Charlotte announced."

Stella and Florence went to Vivian's house to make sure everything was prepared for her when she got home. They cleaned the house from top to bottom. Stella got up early the next morning before Florence and made herself a cup of coffee. Unbeknownst to her friends, Stella always started her day with quiet time, thanking God and counting her blessings. During this morning's quiet time, Stella was watching the rain outside Vivian's kitchen window fall slow and steady, but it was loud enough that she could hear it whisper, *"Be grateful."*

"Thank you, God, for reminding me how very blessed I am. I am dry and warm, can hear and see, and have a wonderful son, good friends, and an endearing family, and I can enjoy a good cup of coffee. I have a purpose in life, no pain, and settled in my spirit, and I am wanting for nothing," Stella prayed.

About that time, Florence came into the kitchen.

"Were you on the phone? Who were you talking to? Some man?" asked Florence sarcastically,

"Not just some man," laughed Stella." "You might say the Man."

"Really?" asked Florence. "When am I going to meet him?"

"I think you already have, but let's change the subject. You think Vivian is going to be able to take care of herself? Her family better step up to the plate, or I am going to release you on them Florence, and they know that they don't want that."

Florence laughed so hard, it brought tears to her eyes.

CHAPTER 25

Time of Transition

D R. JAMES THORNTON had been Dawson's friend for over forty years. He was the best man at Dawson and Charlotte's wedding. She often thought that if she hadn't married Dawson, she would have seriously considered marrying James. He was respectful, athletic, a brilliant surgeon, and a dedicated friend. In fact, Charlotte tried to matchmake him with Stella once, but it didn't seem to progress past one date. Disappointed, Charlotte asked Stella why she did not try to get her hooks into James. In her mind, he was a great catch. Stella smiled and said she earnestly tried, but he was committed to the "other team."

Puzzled, Charlotte asked, "What 'other team' are you talking about?"

Stella looked at Charlotte and asked, "Are you serious?"

"Do you mean James is gay?" asked Charlotte in disbelief.

"Are you kidding me? You mean you never knew? I can't believe you didn't know! I wondered why you dangled that fine man in front of me despite knowing he was unavailable," said Stella laughing. "But I did enjoy trying. He is good company."

When Charlotte answered the phone, she told James that Dawson was not home, and he said he actually wanted to talk with her. He proceeded to confide in Charlotte that Dawson was having some difficulties at work and wanted to know if she had noticed any peculiarities in Dawson's behavior. He seemed to be forgetful and was losing some of his enthusiasm. Since Dawson was his best friend, he felt obligated to make sure everything was okay. He suggested that maybe he just needed a vacation because he knew they hadn't taken one together in years.

Charlotte thanked James for his concern and told him she would pay closer attention to Dawson's behavior. Before he hung up, he asked Charlotte to say hi to her fine friend Stella for him, and they both laughed.

Dawson seemed fine; he was a little absentminded, but she observed nothing else that seemed out of the ordinary. But within two weeks of James's call, Dawson came home from work and announced that he had decided to retire from the hospital and from his medical practice. He said that thirty years of doing the same thing was enough for anyone. He wanted the two of them to travel and enjoy their retirement years while they were young enough and healthy enough to enjoy them. Charlotte was taken by surprise and was flattered that even after all these years, Dawson still wanted to spend time with her, but Charlotte was not sure she was ready to retire. She loved being an operating-room nurse because she felt she was helping people during a critical time of need. Dawson agreed to wait one year for Charlotte to retire, and after that, they would see the world together. In the meantime, he would concentrate on his hobby—woodworking. And since Bella and DJ were married with children of their own, they did not have to be on anyone's schedule.

During the year that Dawson was waiting for Charlotte to retire, his forgetfulness increased, and it was beginning to irritate her. He was spending less and less time on his woodworking hobby. Just ten months ago, she would have had to insist that he come away from the table-mounted router long enough for them to eat dinner. She had tried desperately to convince him that she didn't need another bookcase or boot bench, although she was proud of the pergola that was now the home of her prized Carolina jessamine plant. But now it was like he had lost interest, and he complained that his hands didn't work like they used to. He had always been an avid reader but seemed to have given that up; he said his eyes tired easily now. He even stopped participating in their weekly game of bridge with their neighbors. But what was even more uncharacteristic was the fact that Dawson had developed a full-fledged interest in sex and had begun to secretly watch X-rated channels late at night after Charlotte had gone to sleep. This increased demand for sex had begun to concern Charlotte because it had become hyper and almost aggressive. Not to sell herself short—Charlotte had always been able to hold her own in the bedroom, but as a sixty-five-year-old breast-cancer survivor, her interest and stamina were a little compromised.

On the evening of Vivian's stroke, after Charlotte returned home, she found Dawson already in bed. She kissed him on the forehead, and this roused him from sleep.

"Hi, honey. Did you get supper?"

"Hey, babe. Yes, DJ stopped by with one of his famous dishes, including mushroom risotto. I must say, it was quite tasty. I think there is some left for you. He was so proud of it. How was Vivian?"

"She seems to be doing okay. Florence and Stella will be staying with her for a week, trying to get Jennifer on a schedule. I declare, Vivian took care of that family, and now they can't seem to find time to take care of her. The doctor said there should be no long-term repercussions from the stroke, but she will need to take it easy for a few months. Herman and Jennifer decided that when Vivian is released from the hospital, they will employ a health-care provider to come in a few times a week to help until she gets back on her feet. They can certainly afford it with all that money they inherited from Mrs. Constance," said Charlotte.

"Who is Mrs. Constance?" asked Dawson.

"What do you mean? You know, Vivian's mother-in-law," replied Charlotte.

"Have I met her?" asked Dawson.

It hit Constance like a ton of bricks. She could no longer stay in denial. Dawson was struggling with memory loss.

"Never mind, Dawson. Honey, just go to sleep. We will talk about it tomorrow," said Charlotte as she held back tears.

The next morning, Charlotte called Stella and asked her if she had time for a quick visit. Stella said she could be there in a week. Charlotte had to tell someone and wasn't ready to discuss it with Bella or DJ. She needed to approach this life-changing event with practical preparation and not emotionalism—at least not yet.

One thing about good friends who have a long history with you—they know when you really need them, and nothing else is more important to them during that time than being there for you. As soon as Stella arrived, she hugged Charlotte, and they didn't say anything for a few minutes. Then Charlotte asked her how Jason and Abby were doing in Venice and how she felt about becoming a grandmother.

"Grandma Stella," said Charlotte.

"Wait a minute," said Stella. "Not *Grandma*. That baby has to call me *Duchess*—just *Duchess*," insisted Stella before laughing.

Charlotte poured Stella a cup of the "special coffee" that Stella first made for her.

"You still drinking that coffee, girl?" asked Stella.

"Almost every day, and I owe it all to you," said Charlotte.

As they sipped their spiked coffees, Charlotte unburdened her heart and detailed Dawson's journey away from her.

It seemed like it happened overnight; the light in Dawson's eyes started to grow dim, and his smile faded. His steps were no longer fluid. On one particular evening, as they were having dinner, Charlotte told Stella that she noticed that Dawson's right hand seemed to shake uncontrollably.

Then he started asking questions like "Where are we going to sleep?" and "Whose house is this? It looks just like ours."

Charlotte admitted to Stella that once she stopped running from the truth, a cold chill of acceptance swept over her. Memories of events that she had tried to file away came rushing in like a tsunami. For instance, there was the day when she and Dawson were driving to the mall, and he took his foot off the accelerator right in the middle of traffic because he forgot where they were going; or the time he got up at 3:30 a.m., took a shower, got dressed, and was sitting at the breakfast table, eating his oatmeal; or the time when he asked one evening if his mother had called. "I said, 'Not unless she called from heaven.'"

Charlotte and Stella laughed.

"Stella, Dawson is exhibiting all the classic signs of rapid memory loss—maybe something worse. What am I going to do?"

Stella answered, "Charlotte, you of all people know what you have to do. Just do it."

As soon as she returned home, Charlotte made an appointment with the neurologist for next week, and Stella promised to be there.

When they arrived at the doctor's office, Stella was there, as promised, along with Florence. Vivian would have been there, but she was still recovering, and Florence forbade her to come but promised to let Charlotte know that she was thinking of her and Dawson.

Dawson's diagnosis was confirmed—Alzheimer's disease.

All in all, Dawson and Charlotte took the news in stride since Dawson's mother and uncle had succumbed to the dreaded condition years ago. Bella and DJ provided more comfort to her than she expected. She thought they would fall apart, knowing how much they loved their father, but they made her so very proud. Jason even called her to provide some comfort after Stella told him about Dawson.

Charlotte knew that the lifespan of an average person diagnosed with Alzheimer's disease ranges from four to eight years, but many live well past that. And Dawson was certainly not the average man. But she knew it was past time to organize their future. Almost immediately, Charlotte got to work on helping her husband get through this part of his journey. She researched new medical innovations and treatments for memory loss, contacted current medical experts in the field for their opinions, and relied on her strong faith and true friendships.

Charlotte immediately retired from nursing. She wanted to spend as much time with her husband as possible. They would sleep until they woke up and stayed up until they fell asleep—usually in each other's arms. Both being pragmatic, they had often talked about what the other one would do in the event that one left before the other. Their wills and trusts were in order, and they both gave each other permission with blessings to marry again.

Charlotte recognized when the time came for Dawson to move on. He lived for fifteen years after the initial onset of the disease, only becoming debilitated during the last six months of his life—long enough for Charlotte to say goodbye. This allowed Charlotte enough time to prepare her family and herself to gracefully let go of their physical attachment to Dawson and embrace a more excellent bond that transcended even death. Charlotte grieved as any widow would after losing a husband of thirty-nine years. His death left a deep hole in her heart that she knew would never be filled, but she promised her husband that she would live life as fully as she could and hold close those things that make her happy.

The hardest part of living in that big house alone was the quiet. She would lie in bed at night and thank God for allowing such a sensitive, intelligent, and virile man to find her and walk with her through most of her life's journey. He was a good man, and upon reflection, she realized that he had made her life so easy. She really missed him. She faced the fact that all her married life, she had someone who took care of all her needs. Now that Dawson was gone, she was responsible for all the household chores, like replacing light bulbs, taking out the trash, bringing in the groceries, paying all the bills, filing the taxes, getting the cars inspected, and programming that damned sprinkler system. "Forgive me, Lord," she whispered, and then she started to cry.

CHAPTER 26

When Did You Know You Were Old

I T HAD BEEN over four years since the girls took a vacation out of the country. Traveling requiring navigating through multiple airports at the speed of light and the logistics of making connecting flights were beginning to become more of a challenge than any of them wanted to tackle, even with priority boarding. Traveling when they were young required only an overnight bag with a change of underwear. Now they needed to bring medications, denture containers, extra glasses, a CPAP machine with batteries and collapsible walking canes.

Because of this very thing, these days, their outings consisted of only short stays, rotating between each of their homes. Stella had the privilege of acting as hostess this weekend.

"All right, girls, get your drinks, sit down, and let's start our game," commanded Vivian.

"What is the question this time?" asked Stella.

"We have confessed all our secret sins to each other over the years. What is there left to know? Except I will never tell you all who was sneaking out of my bedroom window on the evening of graduation. I promised to take it to my grave," announced Florence.

"Girl, we have known for years that it was Howard Jackson. He came by to get his jacket that you had fixed for him, and the front door was locked, and he had to climb down the fire escape. We just let you believe that we did not know," confessed Charlotte.

"You crazy b—"

"Don't say it, Florence, with your nasty mouth," warned Stella with a wink.

"Well, I know a question we can ask. Get your drinks, and when someone gives an answer that you agree with, you have to take a drink," volunteered Charlotte.

"Good game, good game. What is the first question?" asked Stella.

"Wait, said Vivian. I don't have my drink yet. You all know I can't move as fast as I used to since I had my stroke."

"That excuse is getting old Vivian. It is not the stroke, you are just getting old, just like the rest of us", laughed Florence.

"Is everyone ready now? Let's start. The question is: When did you finally accept the fact that you are old?" said Charlotte.

"'Old'?" said Stella. "Who's old? Not me. Sixty is the new forty," she said while dancing around.

"'Sixty'? Girl, it has been so long since you were sixty that gray hair is back in style," offered Florence.

"My wine is getting cold, so back to the question. When did you realize you were old?" said Charlotte.

"When the pharmacy clerk automatically applied my senior discount without being asked," smiled Vivian.

And everyone took a drink.

The game continued with one declaration after another:

"When I bought my first pair of Depends."

"When I agreed to get Botox treatments with you all," said Charlotte.

"When you needed Botox treatments," laughed Florence.

"When I bought a wig to cover my thinning hair."

"When I didn't care who saw me with a cane."

"When I looked in the mirror and my mother looked back at me."

"When my stamina and desire to decorate my house for Christmas were gone."

"When I was glad that DJ offered to cook Thanksgiving dinner at his house."

"When I was not insulted when someone got up and gave me their seat."

"When I couldn't remember the secret ingredient of Aunt Eva's bread-pudding recipe."

"When I started preferring hearing from my grandchildren before my children."

"When I started preferring coffee over sex."

They all said, "Amen."

"When I gave up coloring my gray hair."

"Never!" said Stella.

"When they seated me at the head table at the family-reunion banquet."

"When I started reading the obituary section of the newspaper first to check for y'all names," laughed Florence as she pointed around the room.

"When I couldn't eat peppers and onions after 6:00 p.m."

"When the first kindergarten student I taught enrolled her grandchild in my class."

"Really, Florence? Now that's old," laughed Stella.

"Oh, I got one! When the teenage cashier referred to me as "Sweetie." Don't you just hate that?"

A collected "Amen" was expressed.

After numerous glasses of wine were consumed, Stella, Vivian, and even Charlotte were feeling quite cozy, but as usual, Florence was the life of the party. It seemed that the caffeine in the iced tea was beginning to get to her as she started to stumble toward the bathroom. Within two minutes, they heard a loud thump. Florence had fallen to the floor, hitting her head.

After the EMS got Florence to the hospital, the unbelievably young ER doctor diagnosed that she had lost her balance as a result of a bad case of vertigo, but luckily, there was no concussion.

The girls were a little afraid to call the reverend and tell him about what happened to Florence. After he talked with her on the phone, he was reassured that she was fine. He did ask that Florence stay with Stella until he could fly up to drive her back to Atlanta. He didn't want her trying to drive back alone.

"Now that's what you call a real husband," said Vivian. "Howard would have let me drive back in a car with no gas."

And they all had a good laugh.

Charlotte knew it was now or never. She was not getting any younger and did not want to meet her Maker with any unresolved issues.

"Florence, you said earlier that we had confessed all our secret sins to each other over the years. Well, there is one thing I have not confessed," admitted Charlotte.

"We know all there is to know about you, Charlotte," laughed Florence.

"Not all of you," said Charlotte, and then she took a long swallow of her coffee.

She opened up her alabaster box and poured out her pain in the safest place this side of heaven, where she knew that regardless of how her friends felt, she would find understanding and acceptance.

"Remember, after my mother passed, I took an internship in Arizona for six months? You all thought I needed to get away because I was still grieving for my mother. Well, I was really missing her, and I really, really needed her, but I didn't go to Arizona. I went to Colorado. I was not there to attend an internship. I was there to have a baby."

"'A baby'?" asked Vivian.

Florence was speechless.

"Where is the baby? And the baby daddy?" asked Vivian.

"Remember Walter from college? The one who is now the dean of academic affairs at school? That Walter. But he never knew. I never told him. I tried to tell him, but before I could get it out, he excitedly announced that he was engaged. I just couldn't tell him and mess up his life. So I went to Colorado, had the baby, and gave him up for adoption."

Everyone went quiet for at least five minutes.

"But some years ago, Walter finally found out, and the baby grew up and found us both. He forgave us, and we now have a good relationship."

"Where is he? When will we meet him?" asked Vivian.

"You already have," said Stella. "He is Jason—my Jason."

After having their countless questions answered, the four friends embraced one another, and Stella and Charlotte whispered a special "Thank you" to each other.

CHAPTER 27

Decision Time

CHARLOTTE'S MIND DRIFTED to the first Christmas morning she spent without Dawson. Isabela and Dawson Junior were celebrating with their respective families. Memories of Christmases past—when her house was filled with the smell of ginger cookies and the sounds of Christmas carols and children's laughter—played over and over in Charlotte's mind. She knew Bella and DJ would bring the grandchildren by later in the afternoon to share a piece of the traditional rainbow cake and other desserts and bring her presents that she really didn't need.

In an earlier discussion with her friends, Vivian asked, "Why do children think old people want bathrobes and slippers each year?"

"Or foot massagers?" added Stella.

"What about a good bottle of wine or tickets to a jazz festival? I was not born a grandmother, and I really used to be twenty-seven," Charlotte added.

"You know you are preaching to the choir," Stella said.

Charlotte's mind returned to the present.

Charlotte had exactly four weeks to make a selection of which unit at the Manor she wanted. Before she made her final decision, she wanted to get a second opinion, so she asked Vivian to check it out with her. Jack Stewart, the assistant manager, met them. He gave Charlotte the keys to the unit she had selected so she could show Vivian around. Vivian fell in love with the place as well and decided to inquire about availability for herself. As they were headed back to Jack's office, they passed a couple of residents. After they were out of earshot, Vivian asked Charlotte, "Don't these people seem old?"

"How old do you think we are? The minimum age here is sixty-five, and that boat sailed for us at least a decade ago," laughed Charlotte.

"Where is Stella when you need her?" laughed Vivian.

After meeting with Jack, he invited them to stay for lunch to get a feel of the communal dining and observe some of the residents. Jack reminded them that each unit had facilities for cooking, but on days when a resident didn't want to prepare their own meals, the Green House Restaurant was available. They decided to stay for lunch, which was a little disappointing—baked fish and brussels sprouts. Ugh, brussels sprouts!

When Charlotte dropped Vivian home, Vivian had to admit that she really loved the Manor and gave Charlotte her approval.

The next morning, Charlotte submitted her application, made the deposit, and reserved the movers for three weeks. That would give her enough time to finish inventorying her household furnishings and accessories so she could decide which items she could move to her new location and which ones she would part with. She was giving Bella and DJ first choice of things they wanted to retain. She was hoping that they would be civil and not fight over the same items.

Charlotte asked Bella and DJ to meet her at her house so she could tell them she was definitely moving and so they could help her sort out her belongings.

When they arrived, Charlotte discussed her decision to downsize and presented to them where she would be moving. When they realized that their mother had thought through everything, they were in agreement because they were not comfortable with their mother living in that big house alone. They consented to help her sort through the items in the house and select those things they wanted for themselves.

As soon as they began, Charlotte's hairdresser called as said she had a cancellation and if Charlotte could get there in 30 minutes, she could have the reservation. Charlotte accepted the appointment and apologized to her children that she would need to leave for a few hours but while she was gone, if they could tie a red ribbon or put a piece of red tape on everything they wanted, then they would discuss each item when she got back. "Just don't fight over anything." Charlotte then rushed out because she didn't want to be late for the appointment.

It took Charlotte about an hour to return to her house, and when she returned, she saw that Bella and DJ were sitting at the table and devouring some of DJ's famous lasagna.

"Mother, you look beautiful" was the compliment DJ gave her, and Charlotte smiled. How she loved that child—not just because he was the spitting image of his father but because he never missed an opportunity to say something nice.

"Yeah, Mom. Ms. Courtney has not lost her touch," said Isabella. "She went from doing feet to doing hair."

"Well, guys, I don't see many, if any, red ribbons. What were the two of you doing all this time?

If you don't tag what you want today, tomorrow might be too late. Or are the two of you fighting over everything?" asked Charlotte.

Bella looked at DJ, who looked back down at his plate.

"Well, to tell you the truth, Mother, we really don't wa—need anything."

Flabbergasted, Charlotte couldn't believe her ears.

"I can't believe that you or DJ do not want anything. I paid a mint for these furnishings, and these drapes are custom-made. You can't even find window treatments this fine in the stores," said Charlotte, disappointed.

"For you, Mother, they were wonderful, but for me—well, I like a lighter style of decorating," said Bella.

"We did look throughout the house and found a few pieces that we would love, and thanks, Mother, but the majority of the items just don't fit our lifestyles. Just take what you will need, and we will help you dispose of the rest."

"Just tell me what is wrong with these things," said Charlotte.

Both children went through a partial inventory and gave their mother reasons why they declined the household items: the living-room furniture was too heavy and not modular enough; the bedroom-furniture pieces were either too heavy and dark or out of style (after all, they were over thirty years old, and times had changed); the pattern of the custom-designed drapes didn't fit the decor of their houses; the lamps that were imported from India were just too ornate for their tastes; and the electronics were either out-of-date or too cumbersome. They did agree to take all their memorabilia—yearbooks, trophies, awards, etc.—and some books but not the bookcases that their father made; they thought they were too big.

Charlotte was almost in tears. She and Dawson spent a good amount of time trying to properly furnish and decorate the house with the specific idea that their things would be passed on to their children. The desire to fill a home with treasured heirlooms was a hallmark of her generation, but it appeared that the lifestyle of her children's generation did not include it. Charlotte was moving from a 3,500-square-foot, three-level house to a 1,200-square-foot town house in a retirement community. What was she going to do with the furniture that she and her husband had accumulated over the years for their children now that they were too ignorant to want or even appreciate it?

The decision to hire a company to auction off the contents of her house that did not work somewhere else was the best idea. Any item that did not sell would go to charity. Charlotte admitted that if she knew this would happen, she would have spent more money on Botox and less money on the house.

Charlotte was still grateful that Bella had helped her sort through her possessions. She reluctantly had to part with most of them but tried to retain mementos and things that held sentimental value, but the process of choosing which items to bring with her and which ones she would let go was not as easy as she had imagined.

CHAPTER 28

Downsized

"GIRL, YOU DON'T need to move to a retirement home. Just because your kids are grown and gone and Dawson, rest his soul, has moved on doesn't mean it's time for you to be put out to pasture. All you need is another man—someone who can call 911 for you," teased Florence.

Charlotte smiled as she thought of that past conversation.

Well, just because Florence got lucky when she married Rev. Robinson didn't mean Charlotte would become interested in finding another man. As much as she loved Dawson and enjoyed married life, one husband for her lifetime was enough. But after her experience with caring for Dawson and with her children living over four hours away and her advancing age, she knew she needed better immediate access to high-quality health-care services. But her choosing to move into a retirement community was not driven entirely by health concerns. She was not particularly lonely; she enjoyed her own company and had a good network of friends. But she wanted to live life as long as she could—not just exist but live. With Dawson gone, she wanted to be around other people her age who were still as active as she was. She enjoyed dancing, shopping, card competitions, trips to cultural museums, and concerts, especially jazz ones. She wanted to continue contributing to society through charity knitting and serving on civic committees. All these activities, in some form or another, were offered at the Manor.

CHAPTER 29

Moving Day

CHARLOTTE WAS STARTLED back to reality when the phone rang. When she answered it, the voice on the other end was that of Dawson Sr., but he always greeted her with *Honey* and not *Mama*. It was DJ.

"Hey, baby. You sound just like your father," said Charlotte.

"That's the same thing that Bella says when I call her. I take it as a compliment," he admitted.

"Just wanted to remind you that the movers will be there in two hours. Are you ready?"

"As ready as I will ever be," replied Charlotte.

"Don't worry about a thing. I will be there to coordinate the move. You just relax and know that you will go to sleep in a new home. Love you, Mama. See you soon."

And with that DJ was gone.

Charlotte stopped rushing when she retired from her job as an OR nurse. She took her time in everything she did now. She washed her breakfast dishes, packed them and her remaining mementos in her car, and went to her bedroom to get dressed. About that time, DJ and Bella arrived. They pulled rank on their mother and demanded that she leave everything to them. So Charlotte decided to visit her garden one last time while it still was her garden. As she walked the grounds, she said goodbye to the plants and to her life in this space. While she was excited to start a new life in the Manor, it was bittersweet as she had to leave the house and garden with so many memories of times and people gone by. She leisurely walked as she remembered and stopped in front of the butterfly bush that she planted in memory of her mother. As if on cue, a butterfly flew by and alighted on a branch of the bush. Charlotte's mother told her once that the presence of a butterfly is a reminder that you are not alone and that you are moving in the right direction. The butterfly only stayed for a few minutes, and then it flew in the direction of the firepit that Dawson and DJ built and was the scene of numerous backyard barbecues. By the time Charlotte said her goodbyes, Isabella came to the garden and told Charlotte that the movers had cleared out the house and it was time.

CHAPTER 30

New Home, New Life

B Y THE TIME Charlotte drove to her new home, Bella had already had her furniture set up, her clothes hung up in her closet, the kitchen organized and stocked, and her pictures hung. They unpacked her car and found the perfect places for the personal mementos she brought. Once Charlotte was settled, Bella and DJ reversed the roles; they asked their mother to sit down and gave her advice, such as "Keep your doors locked at all times," "Be careful when you talk to strangers," and "Eat all your vegetables." And with that, they hugged their mother real tight, kissed her softly on the cheek, and left. When Charlotte retired to her bedroom, she noticed a gift box on the bed that was addressed to her. She sat down and opened it. It was a photo album named Memory Book with scenes from each room in her old house and of every inch of her garden. While wiping tears from her eyes, Charlotte whispered, "Thank you, God, for a life better than I deserve." As she closed the book and looked around her, she wondered if she would ever feel the same way about her life at the Manor.

The next morning, Charlotte took breakfast in the restaurant so she could meet some of her neighbors. During the following weeks, she discovered that the community was composed of retirees from diverse backgrounds: musicians, housewives, educators, and even nurses. Each occupant had a personal and interesting story. There were some husband-and-wife tenants, but most of them were single or widowed. Charlotte was pleasantly surprised to find that the majority of the residents were still very active—both physically and intellectually.

It took Charlotte only about four weeks to organize a bridge club, of which she was elected president. She even volunteered to teach classes for those who did not know how to play, and within three months, they were having competitions. There were several activities that Charlotte was excited to participate in that kept her as busy as she wanted to be. She found that she had finally settled in at the Manor and began to feel as if she was home. On days when she wanted to be alone, she would retire to her apartment and not have to explain to anyone. When she felt the need to be around people, she would take her meals in the restaurant, join a card game, attend movie night, or even connect with some of the others for an evening out.

It did not take long for Charlotte to invite the girls to come visit for the weekend. They were a little too old to sleep on pallets, but she had two bedrooms, which proved to be enough sleeping spaces to accommodate her friends. Everyone's children were grown, and some of them had children of their own. The friends spent a lot of time sharing pictures of each other's offspring. It was the highlight of each get-together.

Charlotte entertained her children and grandchildren at least three times a year but saw her friends more often. Within five years of Charlotte's moving, Vivian's husband, Herman Washington II, and Rev. Eric Robinson, Florence's husband, had both passed away, and since Stella had been a widow for many years, the four friends were single again. Instead of celebrating each of their birthdays individually, they had one large birthday celebration on February 22 of each year. They chose that date because it didn't conflict with any other celebration and was the day the four of them moved into the same dorm and became friends for life.

During the year they turned eighty-four, Charlotte was doing the entertaining. She looked forward to visits from Stella and Vivian. They spent hours on the telephone, reminiscing about times gone by, sharing recipes (as if they still cooked), telling each other funny stories, and rehashing secrets that they already knew. Playing bridge without Florence made it lose some of its passion, although talking about her always brought smiles to their faces.

"Florence always had an opinion about everything, and she always seemed to relate it to her religion—as if she was the only person who knew God," said Charlotte.

"Remember, she always said she was going home in the Rapture."

"Yeah, but she would add that if she happened to die before Jesus the Christ returned, it would be because of an accident," added Vivian.

"Well," said Stella, "Florence did have that accident."

"And what an accident it was," added Vivian, and then they all laughed as only friends would, given the situation.

Florence had just bought a new dress to wear to her grandson Zachery's wedding and couldn't wait for the girls to see it. She told Charlotte that she liked it so much, she wanted to be buried in it—along with their signature pearls, of course.

One evening, she decided to send Charlotte a selfie of her wearing the dress. She called Charlotte and told her she was sending her a picture but to hold on because she wanted to find the perfect shoes to go with the dress.

After about fifteen minutes, Florence came back to the phone and said, "I found the perfect shoes—the genuine Christian Louboutin pair that I picked up in Paris."

Charlotte yelled, "Florence, you've still got those shoes with the red soles? We were about fifty-five when you bought them. You know they are too high for women our age. Are you crazy? And they are probably dry-rotted!"

"You know these shoes are high quality and do not dry-rot, and besides, they are the only ones that match the pattern of this dress. They still look great, and these are not the really high ones, and they make my legs look good. Wait, I need to get my step stool to get a picture of my whole body so you can see the shoes because the dress is long and you know I have shrunk two inches," said Florence.

As soon as Charlotte finished cautioning Florence to be careful, she heard Florence say, "Got it, and I do look good," and then she heard a loud crashing sound. While trying to get down from the stool, Florence's shoe got tangled in the hem of the dress, and she lost her footing, fell backward, and hit her head on the bedpost. The coroner said she suffered a fatal traumatic brain injury and died instantly.

Florence was able to press Send on her phone before she fell, and the picture was delivered to Charlotte's phone. She did look good in that dress. And yes, she was buried in it, including the shoes.

By this time, they all had experienced the passing of family and friends and had weathered their share of life's disappointments. They finally embraced their wrinkling skin, thinning gray hair, age spots, and skin tags as trophies earned from a life well lived.

Stella remained the consummate actor. Her work with the community theater became legendary. She continued to practice her craft well into her late seventies. But as with all things, the new generation knew little of her performances. Her many awards were displayed throughout her home, and when she had company, she would turn into Baby Jane, playing old videos of past performances and sharing scrapbooks of newspaper and magazine articles featuring her.

Although Vivian suffered a second stroke many years later, which confined her to a wheelchair, her mental faculties were never affected. She had the good mind to protect her fortune from Jennifer and moved to the Manor alongside Charlotte.

Charlotte knew that life had been good to her and humbly accepted the minor physical irritations that accompanied growing old. She never let diabetes or arthritis defeat her. She could still knit, play bridge, and remember the recipe for the mouthwatering gingersnaps that she still made and gifted to all her family and friends at Christmas.

Stella would visit Charlotte and Vivian at the Manor as often as she could, and today was one of those times. They had planned a day of watching old movies and playing cards. Florence's unbridled tongue and high energy were missed especially on days like today. Between hands, the friends would reminisce about fun times they shared through the years and recognized there was never a better group of friends to be found.

Charlotte knew that one day, she, along with Stella and Vivian, would be moving on to that other side of eternity and would find out what Florence had been up to.

"Probably telling Saint Peter not to let us in," laughed Vivian.

But not yet.

The three remaining friends still had a lot of living to do.

In three days, it would be February 22, and they would be celebrating their eighty-seventh birthdays together. Ashton, Jennifer, Isabella, Dawson Jr., and Jason would be coming with their families to help them do it up in the style in which they were accustomed.

Just then, Stella's phone rang. It was Jason. She excused herself and took the call in the next room while Charlotte was pouring each of them another cup of coffee.

When Stella returned, she looked puzzled.

"What's wrong, Stella? What did Jason say?" asked Vivian.

"I'm not sure. They won't be able to make it to our birthday celebration."

"Oh no," said Charlotte. "I was so looking forward to their visit. Why aren't they coming? Couldn't they get a reservation?"

"No, that's not it," replied Stella. "Jason said they had bought their tickets months ago, but their government just canceled all international flights. He said something about a deadly virus that was out of control and spreading. He used the word *pandemic*!"

CPSIA information can be obtained
at www.ICGtesting.com
Printed in the USA
BVHW030111061120
592661BV00002B/2